ABANDONED TO THE NIGHT

THE BROTHERHOOD SERIES - BOOK 3

ADELE CLEE

D1488733

CHAPTER 1

A TAVERN IN SCHILTACH, BAVARIA, 1820

*L*eo Devlin stared out of his bedchamber window at the dimly lit street below. The first faint ripples appeared in the puddles, spots of rain that would soon make the muddy thoroughfare impassable.

Peering out over the canopy of fir trees lining the hills before him, he could see the outline of the castle's conical spire thrusting up towards the heavens. He sneered at the irony of it all. Did the Lord know Satan carried out evil atrocities just a short distance from his door?

With the thick black clouds heralding a heavy downpour, the streets were deserted, abandoned. All the wooden shutters on the windows were closed in anticipation of the storm. His was the only face pressed to the glass, the only one desperate enough not to fear the weather.

The stillness of the night surrounded him, penetrated his clothes to seep into his bones. But his heart had been empty for weeks. Even the fair-haired woman warming his bed had failed to bring the relief he desired.

And he knew who to blame.

Leo glanced over his shoulder at the sleeping maid. It

wasn't the first time he had joined with her. But she had been the last woman he'd taken as a mortal man and consequently he had a burning desire to compare the two experiences. Most amorous encounters were barely memorable, but the memory of the night he'd been turned was seared into his brain—up until the moment the devil woman had spoken her mystical words and sent him tumbling into a deep sleep.

The screech of an owl drew his attention back to the desolate road.

Two nights he had waited for her to come to the tavern. He had laid his trap. Like the night she'd sunk her sharp fangs into his neck, he frolicked with buxom wenches, was openly crude, walked the lonely streets with his usual arrogant swagger.

Nothing.

No sign of his quarry.

He contemplated strolling up to the castle and rapping on the door, act the wandering stranger seeking sanctuary after being caught in the unexpected storm. Would her servants notice the sword strapped to his back? Would they question him, be quick enough to stop him exacting his revenge?

With some reluctance, Leo pushed away from the window. A warrior was only as good as the weapon he wielded. He walked over to the crude wooden bed, stretched his arm out under its base, tapping the dusty boards until his hand settled on the cold metal handle. A frisson of excitement coursed through him as he pulled it out from its hiding place.

The weary maid did not stir.

The slicing sound penetrated the silence as he drew the sword from its scabbard. He held it up to parry with an invisible opponent, twisting his hand to examine the way the blade cut through the air with ease. The candle flame flickered on the reflective surface. The beauty of the polished steel forced him to catch his breath. Leo had fought many men. He'd sliced through linen, scratched skin, but had never cut deep into flesh. Calvino tutored in the art of swordsmanship as a sport, not with the intention of using it as a lethal weapon.

It seemed a shame to sully the metal, to spoil it with her tainted blood.

But he would make the devil woman pay for what she had done. He would do whatever it took to prevent her from building an army of night-walking monsters.

The distant rumbling outside forced him to move back to the window. The thunder sounded more like a growling snarl as the first crack of lightning flashed behind the castle's spire.

Had the Bavarian temptress felt his presence? Did she know of his plan? Could she feel his disdain?

Leo tried to listen for threads of her thoughts, but with his mind plagued by feelings of bitterness and resentment he could barely hear his own internal voice.

A flicker in the corner of his eye caught his attention. This time, the rumbling came from the wheels of a carriage. His heart lurched at the familiar sight. He would know the blood-red conveyance and the black team of four, anywhere. It haunted him during his waking hours. If he were able to sleep, he knew it would appear in his nightmares too.

The woman lying sprawled across his bed yawned. "What time is it?"

"Shush." He strode over to her, stroked her cheek, altered his tone as he repeated, "Go back to sleep. Sleep now." He could not risk the maid seeing the sword. She would be quick to regale the tale of the murderous warrior, and he did not want anyone to know of his private business.

"But I'm not tired."

"Shush. You will sleep now. You will sleep until I wake you."

By the time he returned to the window, the carriage had gone. He punched the air in frustration, only stopping when he noticed the grey shadow of a figure hurrying along the street below. Shrouded in a cloak, the person gripped their hood as they battled against the wind.

The pounding in his chest vibrated in his ears, a gasp catching in his throat as a strand of golden hair whipped around the dark material.

She had come for him.

She had read his thoughts; she knew what he had come to do. The need to maintain her dominance and control was important enough to force her to flee her evil domain and brave the harsh elements.

As he watched her approach the tavern, Leo swallowed down the hard lump in his throat. His hands were shaking; his racing heart caused him to feel dizzy, a little dazed and disorientated. Perhaps he had underestimated his opponent. Perhaps he would be the one to lose his life tonight.

The Marquess of Hartford defeated by a woman?

Never!

Taking deep breaths to calm his agitated spirit, he focused on the importance of his mission. He would avenge his friends, no matter what the cost.

Shrugging into his coat, followed by the leather back harness, he tightened the straps on his shoulders and sheathed his sword before hiding the evidence beneath a full-length cloak.

When she didn't find him sipping his ale would she be bold enough to come up to his room? Then again—

All thoughts suddenly abandoned him. The golden-haired demon walked past the door and continued along the road.

Was it a trap? Was it her intention to lure him away, out into the night? Would she draw him to the graveyard or to another deserted place where she could bare her teeth and control him with her mind?

Either way, he refused to hide in the shadows.

Leo listened for the sensual voice that had once dragged him from the warmth and security of the tavern, the voice that had promised a wealth of pleasure yet delivered nothing but pain. All he could hear was the maid's soft breathing and the muffled din of the rowdy crowd below.

"I'm coming for you," he whispered.

Making his way downstairs, Leo turned his back on the raucous laughter, boisterous antics, and drunken singing. Sneaking out through the back door, he raised the hood of his cloak as he navigated the dark alley. He almost tripped on the stuffed sack until the mound kicked out and delivered a slurred curse.

Slipping out onto the street, he narrowed his gaze, blinking away the droplets of rain clinging to his lashes. He could see her walking ahead. Her strides were quick and purposeful. It took every ounce of restraint he possessed not to charge up to her and take her head clean off her shoulders.

He should have been ashamed to think of harming a woman, let alone in such a callous, vicious way. But the golden temptress was a devil in disguise—not human. She had no heart, no feelings.

When she stopped and rapped on the door of a house, Leo plastered his back against the wall for fear of her spotting him. He waited until she had gone inside before rushing to peer through the tiny gap in the shutters.

Leo didn't know what he expected to find. Perhaps she had woven her mind magic and held some other unsuspecting peer prisoner, her slave to command. Perhaps she was the thirteenth member of a coven and now sat amongst twelve other witches deciding who would be their next victim.

As he gazed through the diamond-shaped hole in the shutter, he almost stumbled back in shock.

Two things disturbed him deeply.

The devil woman had removed her cape. With her hair no longer hidden, the golden tresses hung in glorious waves down her back. She sat in the chair by the fire as a group of children gathered round. One jumped up onto her lap and hugged her tightly.

"And how did you get that bruise?" she said to a boy who pushed to the front to show her his knee.

Leo strained to hear the conversation.

"Frederick pushed me over."

She turned to another boy. "Is this true, Frederick?"

The boy looked at the floor and nodded.

"Then you must be a gentleman. You must hold your head up and say sorry," she replied firmly.

At her command, the boy straightened and delivered his apology with genuine sentiment.

"And what of you, Edwin?" she said. "What must you say to Frederick?"

Edwin gave a gracious bow. "I accept your apology."

"Excellent," she beamed as another child walked towards her carrying a tray of sweet biscuits.

They all watched as his quarry bit into one and swallowed the tiny piece, a host of wide eyes eagerly awaiting her reaction. Whatever she said, it received a joyous cheer from the excited faces.

In a state of utter bewilderment, Leo stepped back.

While he struggled to make sense of it all, he considered the second, most shocking thing. The sight of the golden-haired temptress had caused desire to explode through him like a firework at Vauxhall. The feelings were more powerful, more potent than anything he had ever felt before.

Bloody hell.

As he stepped forward to peer through the window, her gaze drifted to the closed shutters.

She knew he was standing there.

Obviously, she had set a trap, found a way to weaken his position. Devious minds use devious methods, he thought, as he chastised himself for being so fickle. The woman had no heart. Avenging his friends was the only thing that mattered. With a renewed sense of purpose, Leo drew his sword, pressed his back against the wall and waited to confront the golden-haired devil.

CHAPTER 2

"*I*s everything all right, Frau Lockwood?" Herr Bruhn sat down in the chair opposite and shuffled forward to warm his hands by the fire. "You seem preoccupied this evening."

"Forgive me." Ivana forced a smile. Having listened to threads of the old man's thoughts, she knew they were filled with fear—for the children, for money, for his sick wife currently in bed with a fever. "I was just thinking that the children need new shoes, that I must increase your funds this month. The nights are too damp, and we must keep them warm. What of Frau Bruhn? Do you need more help here?"

They were all genuine concerns though they were not what plagued her thoughts tonight.

Someone hovered outside in the shadows.

"You are far too generous, Frau Lockwood. As for Frau Bruhn, she's a strong woman and is determined to fight the fever. Matilda nurses her during the day."

Ivana stared into the flames, lost in the vibrant orange glow. She had heard Herr Bruhn's words, yet another man's thoughts invaded her mind. But like the breathless whispers

8

of the dying, she could not piece together the incoherent sounds.

Herr Bruhn cleared his throat. "Are you well?"

Ivana shook her head, blinked rapidly as she tore her gaze away. "Yes, yes. It is this awful weather. It is not good for the constitution, and I fear the roads will become impassable."

Herr Bruhn raised his chin in acknowledgement. "I often wonder if this is how the Lord delivers his punishment. Perhaps it is his way of culling sinners, those too weak to survive the harsh conditions."

A sudden chill passed through her.

"A man with a heart as huge as yours should have nothing to fear." Ivana would always be indebted to the couple for giving the children a secure, loving home. "I am certain Frau Bruhn will make a speedy recovery."

A strange sense of foreboding settled around her. Perhaps Herr Bruhn was right, and these odd voices in her head, coupled with the heavy tension hanging in the air, were signalling the demise of a sinner. Her demise.

"Then neither of us have anything to fear," Herr Bruhn said confidently.

Ivana smiled again, despite the fact that wasn't entirely true.

They were silent for a moment until Ivana said, "I shall arrange for someone to relieve Matilda for a few hours each day. The child needs exercise, to breathe clean air, to focus on her studies."

Herr Bruhn clasped his hands together and held them to his chest. "That would be wonderful, as would the offer of new shoes and heating expenses. I cannot thank you enough for your kindness."

"It is I who should thank you. Without your tireless efforts, heaven knows what would have happened to the children." She inclined her head out of respect. "I am eternally grateful." She glanced at the window, drawn to the closed shutters. "And know, if anything should happen to me, provisions have been set aside for their care."

Herr Bruhn shook his head vigorously as tears formed in the corner of his eyes. "You are an angel, Frau Lockwood, sent to ease our woes."

The man would think differently if he witnessed the sharp fangs overhanging her bottom lip, if he stared into eyes blacker than the night, saw her drink blood.

Ivana stood, feeling an urge to distract her overactive mind. "I shall go and read to the children, tuck them into their beds while you sit in peace and eat your supper. And thank you for allowing me to come when the hour is so late."

In the winter months, she came earlier and spent the whole evening with them. In the summer months, Herr Bruhn knew her duties at the castle monopolised her time—unless the weather brought clouds thick enough to obscure the sun.

"They would not wish to miss your nightly visits," he said to reassure her. "It is only nine. Lately, they rarely rise before eight."

During the time spent regaling tales of errant knights and distressed damsels, she struggled to forget about the mysterious stranger lurking outside in the shadows. At some point, she would have to leave the Bruhn household. Only then would his identity be revealed to her. Only then would she know why the man wished to do her harm.

Odd threads of his thoughts had interrupted her medieval tale, ruined the joy she gleaned from playing mother to the innocent. Hatred and loathing were the overriding emotions she felt from him. Bitterness and resentment were buried somewhere within, too.

Descending the stairs, she took a deep breath to regain her composure before entering the small parlour.

"They are all sleeping soundly," she said, feigning a serene smile. "Well, so they would have me believe."

Herr Bruhn nodded from his fireside chair. "I shall go and look in on them in a short while. Will you stay for supper?"

Ivana shook her head. It had taken all her strength not to choke on the sweet biscuit. But she could not refuse the children anything. "Another time, perhaps. I should get home before the road becomes a flowing torrent of muddy slush." Her gaze flicked to the window. "Sylvester will call by tomorrow and bring the funds you need."

Herr Bruhn shot to his feet and followed her out into the hall. "God bless you, Frau Lockwood."

Ivana took her cape from the coat stand, draped it around her shoulders and tied it firmly at the neck. "And may he bless you, Herr Bruhn," she said, choosing not to raise the hood as she must be alert this evening. As she moved towards the door, she felt the stranger's anxiety, felt the torment raging in his heart.

I have come for you.

The words rebounded back and forth in her mind.

It could mean only one thing—one of the gentlemen had returned.

But which one?

"Before I leave, may I use some paper and your ink pot?"

Herr Bruhn nodded. "Of course, of course. Come this way."

Ivana followed him to a room that had once been the man's study, a place to relax, to enjoy the solitude. Now, it served a multitude of functions: playroom, schoolroom, a place to dry wet boots.

"Over here." Herr Bruhn rushed to the desk, set about

clearing away letters, books, brushed the dust away with his sleeve. "You'll find paper in the drawer and ink in the pot. Use what you will." Offering a bow, he shuffled backwards. "I shall leave you in peace."

Ivana needed but a minute to complete her task. Blowing on the scrawled note, she went in search of Herr Bruhn.

"In case there should be any doubt," she said, handing him the paper.

He scanned it quickly, glanced up at her and then read it again.

"It is proof of the provisions I have made for the children," she continued. "Should Sylvester not call tomorrow with the funds you need, you are to seek him out and present this letter to him."

The man stared at her, a frown marring his brow. "You are making me nervous. Are you sure you are not ill? Are you leaving, going away somewhere?"

Ivana placed her hand on the man's arm. "No. I am not ill and you know I would never leave the children." She gave a light chuckle to ease his fears. "With the storm, the roads are treacherous. One never knows their fate. My only concern is to know that you have everything you need."

Herr Bruhn appeared mildly satisfied with her explanation.

"Now," she continued, wrapping her cape firmly across her chest. "I must be on my way."

The old man walked her to the door. "Sylvester *is* waiting for you?" he asked, his tone revealing his concern.

"He is." Herr Bruhn knew she liked to walk for a few minutes, and that she rarely brought the carriage into the village. When one lived for the night, one took every opportunity to feel free, to feel normal. "He will be waiting in his usual place."

She doubted she would get far before the hunter struck. There was no point putting off the inevitable. She had always known the day would come. Indeed, she had expected one of them to come much sooner. The passing years had given her a false sense of security, but she would soon know of his intention.

As soon as Herr Bruhn opened the door, the wind came rushing in, blowing her hair about her face, causing her to wince as she stepped over the threshold. "Quickly, shut the door behind me." She sounded breathless, perhaps even a little fearful. The stubborn man refused to listen, holding the door a foot away from the jamb. "Please, Herr Bruhn." She did not want him to witness her demise. "I cannot leave here until I know you're safely inside."

Herr Bruhn nodded. "Hurry home," he said as he closed the door. "Be safe."

Ivana contemplated raising her hood as the wind whistled about her ears, biting at her cheeks until they stung. The rain had stopped momentarily, but the thunder still grumbled and groaned in the distance.

I know you're there.

She sent her silent message as she continued down the deserted road. Ivana sensed him walking behind her before she heard the sound of footsteps, before the sudden rush of emotion filled her chest. The hunter was in pain. A deep level of anguish permeated his thoughts. He felt lost and alone— had masked it all with anger and resentment.

Guilt flared, and she chastised herself for being so fickle.

The gentleman had deserved his punishment. The thought gave her the courage to confront her quarry and without any warning, she swung around to face him.

It was difficult to make him out in the darkness. With every shutter on every window closed, there was an absence of light spilling out onto the street. It didn't help that he wore a thick black cloak, his face hidden in the depths of the hood.

"I did wonder which one of you would have the courage to return," she said with an arrogance she only used with those she despised. With her attention drawn to the blade in his hand, she added, "If you're going to kill me, at least afford me the courtesy of seeing your face."

Don't let it be him.

The words raced through her mind as the hunter stepped closer.

"Courtesy?" He stood just a few feet away. "Were you so generous of spirit when you took our humanity?"

She could see the sculptured line of his jaw, the full lips that formed the bitter words, just the tip of his nose peeking out of his black shroud. The sense of familiarity was strong. But their affinity for the night would always bind them together.

"You will show me your face. You will not refuse me." She drew on her ability to coax and persuade. He would try to fight it, of course, but would he be strong enough to disobey? Either way, she would not rest until she knew the name of her quarry.

"Do not think you can control me," he sneered. "Do you think I will bend so easily to your will?"

Ivana smiled. No matter how strong, no matter how skilled in mind control, surely she would have an advantage. She had taken his blood, let it mingle with her own, let him suck from her pricked finger. Even if she did possess the strength of will to prevent him from taking her life, was this not the moment she had been waiting for?

Wasn't death the thing she had been craving?

"Lower your hood." Her icy tone sliced through the volatile air. The wind howled around them, swirling about their clothes, pushing, pushing in a bid to whip them away. "I will see your face."

"In this, I will not fight you." Confidence and arrogance infused his tone. "Perhaps you should know the face of the man come to put an end to your devilish deeds. Perhaps you should look upon the face of the man whose life you have ruined."

The hunter tugged at his hood.

Ivana held her breath.

No! Not him!

It took a moment to drink in his features, for her mind to accept the vision standing before her. If God had sought to punish her, he had chosen wisely. Very wisely, indeed.

Leo!

His name echoed through her mind, over and over.

Why him? Her hands were shaking, the pain in her heart unbearable. Why not one of the others?

"Well?" He gave a disdainful snort. "Do you remember me? Do you recall the night you created a monster?"

The heavens opened in response; the first few drops of rain suddenly turned into a streaming torrent, saturating them in seconds.

Neither moved.

"Of course I remember you." How could she ever forget? She had thought of him many times. She had broken her own set of rigid rules. Not that he would remember. "Welcome home, Leo."

With anger and bitterness etched on his face, he cried, "This place is not my home."

"It is the place of your birth, is it not?" she replied calmly. "Your rebirth. You are not the same man who came here three years ago."

Her heart lurched when she thought of how slowly time

had passed, how long it was since she had last seen his handsome countenance.

"No! I am not the same man. You destroyed him out of spite or for some other twisted reason."

"And I am glad of it," she yelled. She was starting to let her emotions control her. Wiping away the rivulets running down her face, she exhaled slowly.

She would not fight him. She could not tell him the truth.

The time had come.

He could have what he wanted—a chance to rid himself of the bitterness. A chance for revenge. Pulling the ties on her cape, she let the sodden garment fall to the ground.

"I am glad it is you who came," she said, remembering the earthy taste of his skin. Holding her arms wide, she glanced up at the heavens and blinked away the droplets. "Forgive me," she whispered. "But know that everything I did, I did for them."

"What are you saying? Is it a spell? Are you rousing your demon army to come slay me where I stand?"

Ivana ignored his incessant questions.

"Punish me. Protect them." A sense of relief pushed to the fore. The rain had come to cleanse her, to wash away her sins. Despite the gravity of her situation, she felt oddly calm. She sucked in a deep breath and closed her eyes. "I am ready now. Do what you have come to do. Do what you will."

Set me free.

CHAPTER 3

*L*eo stared at the golden-haired devil and had to admit she looked more like a celestial being; one of God's heavenly angels waiting for the clouds to part so she could be spirited home.

Damn it.

With her arms stretched wide, her face glistening with a radiant sheen as the raindrops slipped from her skin, her dress clinging to the soft curves of her body, he knew he did not have the strength to carry out the evil task.

She lowered her head and stared at him. "Why the delay? Do you plan to wait until you see a glimmer of hope flash in my eyes? Is it your intention to torture me?"

Torture?

If she believed this to be torture, then the woman had no real concept of the word. Loneliness plagued him. A feeling of utter hopelessness was his constant companion now. The pain lingered. It festered inside with no hope of an end in sight. That was the most brutal punishment of all.

Leo wiped his hand on his thigh then gripped the handle of his sword with both hands. One mighty swing and he would take her head from her shoulders. Clean. Easy. It would be an act of retribution, a way of restoring the balance. It would be a way of making her pay for all the agonising nights spent craving blood. It would be recompense for the nights spent glaring longingly at the pulsing vein in a pretty debutante's neck, knowing he could never truly satisfy the need clawing away inside.

Justice was all he wanted, for Elliot: his brother and friend. Justice for Alexander and for all those forced to live with the restrictions brought about by the terrifying affliction. And so, with a renewed sense of determination he took a step forward, drew a deep breath and raised the sword.

The heartless creature before him offered a reassuring smile—a smile of all things—then raised her head to the heavens once more.

"Bless the children," she whispered, but he heard the words rebound back and forth in his mind. "In my absence, keep them safe. Protect them always."

The children?

Did she mean the children she had used to deceive him, to cause doubt and uncertainty to take hold? For a moment, he might have believed she cared about something other than her need to steal the souls of mortal men. Why would a woman, sent to do the Devil's work, pray for the Lord's assistance?

Leo lowered the sword once again. A sudden urge to understand her motives gripped him. "Tell me. Tell me why you turned me into the monster you see before you. Tell me why you sought to rob me of my humanity."

The golden-haired temptress glared at him. "Will you not just get it over with. I am tired, cold and soaked to the skin. At the moment, death seems quite a pleasant option, and I have no desire to talk anymore." Her weary gaze drifted over him. She opened her mouth to speak, hesitated, then said,

"But know that you earnt the right to be chosen. Know that you had a part to play in it all."

The woman spoke in riddles to confuse him. "That explains nothing." He wanted an answer to the question haunting him. This was to be his only opportunity to make any sense of it. "Why me? I need to know why you chose me out of all the men passing through here."

Not just him. Why had she chosen Elliot and Alexander? Were there more gentlemen wandering the world suffering with the same debilitating affliction?

She narrowed her gaze, dropped her hands to her side. "You mean you don't know? You do not remember? Do you not have the faintest suspicion? Have you not come to the obvious conclusion?"

Leo wiped the water from his face and flicked the excess liquid from his hand. "Would I have asked if I did?"

"Have you not replayed the events of the night over and over in your mind?" she asked incredulously. "Have you not examined them hoping to stumble upon your mistake, your error of judgement?"

Leo gave a disdainful snort. "I have lived the nightmare over and over again for the last three years. I have dissected every word spoken, every deed and action. But still, it makes no sense. My mind is like a dark, empty cavern whenever I think of what happened that night."

She shook her head and cast him a look that spoke of contempt. But another emotion flashed briefly in her eyes: compassion, perhaps pity. "Then I cannot help you. You must kill me, or you must leave here. You do not—"

"Frau Lockwood. Frau Lockwood."

Suddenly her gaze shot beyond his shoulder, and she muttered a curse. "Now look what your dithering has done."

His dithering? She made it sound as though she wanted him to put an end to her life.

"Say nothing to him," she continued through gritted teeth. "He has no idea what we are. He would be frightened, confused. He would not understand."

Leo glanced behind at the old man tottering along the street, holding a coat above his head to protect him from the rain. "If I abide by your request, what will you do for me in return?"

Her eyes widened, and she shook her head. "You would blackmail me for my desire to protect an elderly man's feelings? Good Lord, you really are a monster."

The words were like barbed arrows piercing his heart. He knew what he was. He did not need the woman responsible for his depraved condition to remind him. Dismissing his irritation, he decided to use the situation to his advantage.

"Tell me what I want to know about the night you sunk your filthy fangs into my neck, and I will keep your secret." Leo gave a satisfied smirk as it felt good to have the upper hand. "I would hate to reveal the true nature of my affliction. And I doubt his heart would take the shock."

She sucked in her cheeks as she glared at him. "Is that the price of a man's sanity? Do you have no shame?" She shook her head and sighed. "Very well. What choice do I have?"

"None. But I will have your word."

"Then you have it." She barged past him and rushed towards the old man. "Herr Bruhn, you must go back inside. You'll catch a chill out here in this dreadful weather."

The old man squinted and blinked rapidly. "Is everything all right? You're soaked through. What has happened to your cape? Why have you not gone home?" He tried to use his coat to shield her from the rain as his concerned gaze fell to Leo's sword. "What ... what is going on here?"

"All is well, Herr Bruhn." She put her hand on his back and steered him away. "There is a problem with my carriage. The road is impassable, and I must walk home. This gentleman has been instructed to ensure I reach there safely."

The man glanced back over his shoulder. "But who is he? I have never seen him here before."

With some difficulty, Leo placed his sword back in the harness. "Herr Bruhn." He inclined his head to the old man. It suddenly occurred to him that he didn't know her name. In the years when he had cursed her and wished for her demise, he knew her only as the golden-haired devil. "I have been instructed to protect the lady," Leo said, struggling to form the only polite word he knew of to describe the woman standing in front of him. "But you must go inside. If we do not leave now, I fear we will struggle to make it back, even on foot."

"Herr Bruhn, I cannot afford for you to be ill too," she implored.

Leo wondered why she did not use her skill for persuasion to force the man back into his home. Well, if she wouldn't do it, he would.

"You must go inside, Herr Bruhn. You must go inside now." Leo's tone was firm, commanding and the golden-haired devil shot him an irritated glare.

"I must get inside," he said, shuffling towards a house on their right. "You are certain you will make it home safely?"

"I am certain," she replied. "I need you to be well. I need you to take care of the children. And I need to hurry home and get out of these wet clothes. Sylvester will be along to see you tomorrow."

Placated, Herr Bruhn nodded vigorously. They escorted him to his door, bid him goodnight and then simply stared at each other.

"Well?" She thrust her hands on her hips as soon as Herr Bruhn closed the door. The wet garment clung to her womanly curves, enhanced the shape of her perfectly round breasts and Leo groaned inwardly.

"Well, what?" he snapped, agitated by his reaction to her shapely figure. Damn it all. He had spent years lusting after women. To some extent his cock possessed a mind of its own, responded to the female form as opposed to the character of the woman within.

"Are you going to kill me where I stand or are you coming with me?"

Leo jerked his head back. "Coming with you where?"

An image of the forest flooded his mind, quickly followed by the dark, suffocating confines of her carriage, and the stone stairs curling up to the demon's chamber.

A smile touched the corners of her lips, but it did not reach her eyes or illuminate her face. "I dislike lying to Herr Bruhn. You will escort me home. We will change out of these wet clothes, drink to suppress our hunger. I will tell you what you need to know, and you will decide what you wish to do with me."

She was not using manipulation to persuade him to follow her, but as she sauntered past him, he felt a tug deep in his gut that forced him to traipse along behind.

Christ, if Elliot were here, he would think him fit for Bedlam. Indeed, in the hours he had waited at the window of the tavern hoping to catch sight of her, he could never have predicted this was how the night would end.

The tavern!

"Wait," he cried, remembering the maid he had instructed to sleep until he told her otherwise. "I'll be but a minute." They would find her in his room and believe he had administered poison, or an opiate to drug her into submission.

She stopped, picked her sodden cape off the ground and shook it out. "My carriage is waiting further along the road. I shall wait for you inside."

Leo swallowed down his surprise. She could have climbed into her conveyance and sent the horses bolting for home. He would never catch up with her. He would never reach her once she'd passed through the iron gate of her fortress.

He nodded and then made his way back up to his room. The water running from his clothes left a slippery trail across the wooden boards. Giving the maid a vigorous shake and a command to wake, he was gone before she had a chance to sit up and rub the sleep from her eyes.

Pushing through the wind and rain, Leo continued along the deserted street. The thin streams of light escaping through the shutters did little to illuminate his way. The hulking black shadow of her carriage loomed into view. He could have been invisible and still the coachman, sitting muffled in his greatcoat, could not have paid him any less attention. An attempt to listen to his thoughts proved futile, and if it had not been for the twitch of a finger on the reins, Leo would have staked his life the man was a sitting corpse.

Leo paused at the carriage door. A sudden sense of fore-boding gripped him, and he pulled his sword from its back harness and held it at his side. Elliot's voice echoed through his mind. The voice of logic and reason reminding him it was sheer folly to climb into her conveyance.

But Leo had nothing left to lose.

He had lived the same nightmare every day, made all the worse since Elliot found love. The woman's curse had left him alone, abandoned to the night that had so cruelly claimed him. The escapades of the brotherhood would become a distant memory, leaving him no choice but to forge ahead, to carve a new life for himself.

Do you intend to stand in the rain all night?

Her words penetrated his chaotic thoughts. She did not frighten him. Not anymore. Nothing she could do to him could be worse than the hell he was already living.

Sensing his decision, she opened the door for him, and he climbed into the one place he thought never to see again. As soon as he slammed the door shut, the carriage lurched forward. He fell back into the seat, his hand still gripping the handle of his sword.

"I shall make sure you're given a big enough bed so you may sleep with it as well." Her amused gaze travelled down the length of the steel blade.

"Sleep? Are you trying to provoke me? You know I haven't slept a wink since you pricked my neck with your sharp fangs. Besides, I have no intention of staying that long."

She gave a low chuckle. "We shall see. One never knows where the path of fate may lead."

"You say that as though you have the ability to predict the future."

"More the ability to remember the past." She reached for the blanket at her side, used it to dry her cheeks and pat the ends of her hair. "None of us know what the future holds. Surely experience has taught you that. Did you expect that a drunken night of debauchery would see you cursed for eternity?" Her gaze drifted over him. He saw something akin to regret, perhaps disappointment reflected there. "Indeed, like you, I am fully aware of the price one pays for naivete, for being so weak and insipid."

Leo gave a contemptuous snort. "I would hardly call you weak and insipid."

"You do not know the first thing about me." Her tone was sharp, and he felt a sudden stab of pain, a fragment of fear he sensed lay buried beneath her calm facade.

"I know you enjoy ripping out the hearts of men." A gust of wind shook the carriage as it climbed the narrow path cutting up through the trees. Leo put both hands on the handle of his sword to steady his balance. "I know revenge burns brightly within you, and so you seek to destroy other people's lives as a way of exerting control."

She glanced out of the window, stared at the passing shadows. "As I said, you know nothing about me. But I will keep my word. Soon, all will be revealed."

CHAPTER 4

*I*n the close confines of the carriage, Ivana studied him. It was obvious he remembered little about his time with her—just as she had intended. All about them, the air whirled with palpable tension. She tried to read his thoughts, to delve deeper to discover what other feelings lay buried beneath the hatred and anger.

But something stopped her.

One could not know a person from listening to the random musings of the mind. And she was curious to learn more about him. Was he so different from the man who had left her three years ago? Had she made a mistake in poisoning his blood? Or in battling with his affliction had he found humility?

Despite his eagerness to sever her head from her shoulders, she believed he had lost the brash, overbearing manner that had first captured her attention. In itself, it was a step towards redemption.

"We're approaching the gates." Her words penetrated the uncomfortable silence, and they rattled across the bridge before rushing through the stone arch leading into the court-yard. "Do you remember being here?"

She hoped the answer was no. But a small part of her wanted to see his eyes flash with the same fiery passion that had once warmed her heart.

He inhaled deeply. "I have a vague recollection, but despite numerous efforts to piece together the events of that night the memories are fragmented."

Ivana smiled. She remembered every minute detail of his time at the castle. The fact he recalled very little gave her an advantage. "I've heard it said that to visit the scene of one's nightmares can often prompt visions, images of memories locked away."

Would he recall the scent of her skin or the taste of her blood?

Something akin to fear flashed in his brown eyes and then he blinked, and it was gone. "For your sake, I hope you're wrong. If it's as horrific as I imagine, I'll not be responsible for my actions."

"Oh, I think you'll be pleasantly surprised."

The carriage rumbled to a halt, swayed back and forth as Sylvester jumped down from his seat to open the door.

"After you." Ivana waved her hand as Sylvester lowered the steps. "I know how susceptible you are, how easily you give in to temptation, and I would not wish to have a sword thrust in my back."

"You think you have the measure of me," he scolded. "You should know I'm no coward."

"Did you not just sneak up behind me with the intention of ending my life?" she said, rising to alight first. She accepted Sylvester's hand, glanced back at Leo. "Did you not hide your face in the depths of your hood?"

Ivana felt his irate glare whipping across her shoulders.

But she did not give him an opportunity to reply. She turned to Sylvester. "I need you to do something for me in the morning. Herr Bruhn is expecting you to call. I shall leave a package for him on the desk in the study."

Sylvester inclined his head. His gaze flitted to her companion although it wasn't his place to pass comment. "Consider it done."

A hulking figure of a man, her servant was one of the few people she turned to for support. His loyalty had been put to the test many times over the years, and he had never failed her.

Ivana tugged Sylvester's sleeve and pulled him further away from the carriage. "He is angry," she whispered, "that is all. Do not worry about the sword. He has no intention of using it."

"Is he as strong as you?"

With concern etched on his face, Ivana did not have the heart to tell him she had come close to losing her life. "No. I am able to manipulate his thoughts," she said, even though she doubted the truth of it.

"And he remembers nothing of his time here?"

"No. Nothing."

Sylvester craned his neck, a movement he often used to suppress his frustration. "You will call me if you need me?"

Ivana offered a reassuring smile. "Of course." If Leo made a sudden decision to use his sword, she would not have time to scream. "Ask Julia to draw a bath, and I'd be grateful if you would prepare a room for our guest."

Sylvester eyed the man behind her with some suspicion. "How long will he stay?" Recognising the impertinence in his tone, he added, "I will need to inform Frau Hermann that we'll need more blood."

Ivana considered the question. The answer would depend

on whether he accepted her motive for turning him, whether he accepted she had a justifiable reason.

She shrugged. "Perhaps an hour." The image of her headless body lying sprawled in a pool of blood flashed into her mind. "Perhaps a night."

The thought of a night spent knowing he was close caused panic to flare, and she quickly dismissed it.

Sylvester sighed. "To let him stay longer than that would be dangerous."

Ivana nodded. "I know."

"Shall I take his sword?"

"No." She shook her head while attempting to give a confident smile. "Beneath the bravado he has a fear of being here. Let him keep his weapon if it brings him comfort."

It could well be a decision she would regret.

Sylvester nodded and moved to walk away.

"Tell Herr Bruhn all is well," she said. When warming her cold bones in her tub, she would attempt to send peaceful thoughts to the old man. He needed his rest and could not spend the night lying awake worrying. "Tell him I shall call to see him tomorrow evening."

A gust of wind breezed over her, the wet gown clinging to her body, and she shivered as though shrouded in a sheet of ice.

"We should go inside." Ivana turned to her guest who was standing in the courtyard staring up at the parapets. "Sylvester will escort you to your chamber and find something dry and suitable for you to wear. We shall continue our conversation in the Great Hall when we reconvene in an hour."

He glanced down at his sodden cloak, patted the material moulded around his muscular thigh. "I shall accept your hospitality but only because I want to hear the truth from your lips. Because I owe it to my brothers to provide them with an explanation for the misery you have caused."

His brothers?

She inclined her head. "I understand. Have no fear. You will receive the information you seek. It may surprise you to learn I would never break an oath. Indeed, without honour and integrity, we have nothing."

Leo raised a cynical brow. "Save the preaching for someone more inclined to believe you."

"You might change your mind about me. Then again, you might not." Ivana simply smiled as she walked past him. "I must take a bath. Sylvester will see to your needs."

"Wait." Leo caught up with her as she approached the large oak door, placed his palm flat against the studded surface in a bid to prevent her from entering. "Despite all you've said, I do not trust you. I'll not leave your side while I'm here."

"What?" she snorted incredulously. "Do you intend to watch me bathe?"

The question caused a frisson of desire to ripple through her, an odd sense of excitement at the prospect of teasing him. It had been three years since she had felt the warm glow of passion ignite—three years since he had awakened a feeling she thought was lost to her.

"I intend to remain at your side until you have told me what I want to know," he said coldly, but it did not dampen her ardour. "Only then shall I reassess my position. Only then shall I decide what to do with you."

Something in his tone caused the hairs at her nape to spring to life. The shiver running down her back had nothing to do with the biting wind.

"Do what you will," she replied, keeping her voice calm and even. She glanced at the sword he'd replaced in its harness. "Under the circumstances, I am hardly in a position to protest."

Leo dropped his hand and gestured to the door. "Then lead the way," he said with a hint of contempt.

Ivana led him up the curved stone staircase to the tower chamber, aware of his sudden intake of breath. "Do you recall coming up here?" She was curious to know what he remembered.

"I have seen these stairs many times in my dreams." He made an odd puffing sound. "While I no longer sleep, my mind still drifts, still wanders. I often see images dancing before my eyes."

She entered her chamber, but he lingered in the doorway.

"You may come in. I'll not bite you again."

"Am I supposed to be amused by your comment?" With hesitant steps he walked into the room, moving to look out of the large arched window. "Is this where you stand and search for your victims?" he said, pointing to the cluster of rooftops below.

"No." She moved behind the dressing screen as Julia and Sylvester entered carrying buckets of water. "Many English aristocrats and noblemen pass through here eager to experience the beauty of the forest before heading down into Switzerland and Italy. Some call it a *Grand Tour*, but there is nothing *grand* about the way they behave."

He made no reply and remained silent while her servants filled the tub.

She came around the screen wearing her robe, her damp hair hanging loosely around her shoulders. "I had to look no further than the local tavern to find men worthy of my disdain."

His head shot round, his furious glare softening a little when he observed her relaxed attire. "What gives you the right to judge? What gives you the right to play with the lives of innocent men?"

Julia stepped forward and held on to the robe to protect Ivana's modesty as she stepped into the tub. Her maid had travelled with her from London many years ago. The grey hairs at her temple were a constant reminder of her mortality and it broke Ivana's heart to think of a life without her companion.

"Oh, I believe I have earned the right to punish those with no regard for the welfare of others." Ivana swished the warm water over her arms. "I act on behalf of those without a voice. And I would hardly call the men innocent."

Glancing up, she caught his heated gaze, heard the ragged sound of his breathing. Muttering a curse, he turned to the window. "Then tell me what I did to force your hand. Tell me why you chose me to be the recipient of such a wicked curse."

Ivana touched Julia's hand as she wiped her shoulders with the wet cloth. "Leave us. I shall be all right here on my own."

Julia's thin lips were lost in a grimace. "I will wait outside should you need me."

Ivana nodded. "Leave the linen towel on the floor. Close the door and do not enter unless I call for you."

As soon as the door met with the jamb, Ivana stood up. The sound of water cascading from her limbs caused Leo to turn around, his eyes growing wide at the sight of her naked body.

Ivana had no shame—not anymore.

The children's welfare was the only thing that mattered to her.

As she stepped out of the tub, she ignored his foul-mouthed rant, his garbled demand for decency. But all words and actions held some purpose or meaning for her. Leo's lustful glare confirmed he still battled the demons within. It confirmed that his memories of her were not lost, only buried.

"What?" she mocked as she stood by the fire and dried her body with the towel. "Are you not familiar with the female form? Were you not the one who insisted on staying while I bathed?"

He moved to turn away, yet she could hear the restless sound of his chaotic thoughts.

With an arrogant curl of the lip and a stubborn stance, he faced her fully. "You're right. It is nothing new to me. Nothing I have not seen a hundred times before."

Despite his desperate attempt to demean her, she took no offence. "Exactly," she said, noting how his wandering eyes betrayed him, how easily they revealed the truth he would not speak. "You should change out of your wet clothes. Sylvester has put a shirt and breeches on the bed, and you're welcome to bathe in my water."

He glanced at the copper vessel; inevitably the thought of relaxing his cold and tired muscles proved too tempting to resist. "Very well." Even in those two little words, his tone held a supreme confidence in his ability to overthrow her in this battle of wills. "But I'll keep the sword with me."

"I can leave the room if you'd prefer."

"No. You will stay where I can see you."

On her part, it was another test.

Stripping him bare would create a certain vulnerability, a realisation that they were merely people: flesh and bone, living, breathing. He would remember this moment if he ever dared to wield his weapon.

Of course, it would also give her the opportunity to test her resolve. Would his body be as magnificent as she remembered? Would she be just as eager to break the oath she had made before God?

Ivana slid the loose white gown over her head and then sat down on the bed to brush her hair. "Shall I ask the servants to move the dressing screen? It will allow you a little privacy."

He snorted as his black cloak fell to the floor. "You've drunk my blood, ripped my soul from my body. You've taken everything I have. What need is there for me to hide away in the shadows?"

She had not taken everything. Some things he had given freely.

"We have shared much," she said, watching him unbuckle the leather straps at his shoulders. "Things you do not remember."

When his linen shirt joined the cloak on the floor, she drank in the sight of his broad chest, her gaze focusing on the branding she'd had no choice but to burn into his chest. The muscles in her core pulsed; her heart was beating so fast she struggled to swallow.

She had felt this way about him from the beginning.

When he unbuttoned his breeches, she tried to feign indifference. But his arrogant gaze met hers as the garment slithered down over his hips.

Ivana could not suppress the soft moan that left her lips as lascivious images of the nights they had spent together flooded her mind. Desire burst bright inside. She wanted him —just as she had wanted him on that first foggy evening three years ago.

"You are just as I remember," she said before running her tongue over her teeth for fear her fangs would protract, for fear she would drain him dry as she took him into her willing body.

"Once again, you appear to have an advantage," he said as he climbed into the tub and bent his knees to let the water lap his shoulders.

"Then perhaps it is only right I even the odds, so to speak."

Ivana ignored the voice of reason telling her she was out of her depth, telling her that to reveal anything was sheer folly. Utter madness. But lust clawed away at logic. She focused her thoughts, roused the image of him lying naked on her bed, relived the moment he had thrust inside her for the first time.

A pleasurable groan escaped from his lips as his head fell back against the copper rim. She looked over at him, conveyed the true depth of the passion she had experienced at his hands—almost lost herself in transferring the erotic memory.

"What are you doing to me?" he groaned, relinquishing control to the power of her mind as she let him feel the emotions they had shared upon finding their release. "Oh, God. Why ... why am I seeing this?"

"I am giving you a taste of what happened here. I am letting you see it was not all as horrifying as you believed it to be."

He shot up, water spilling out onto the floor. "It is some sort of evil trick," he spat yet his eyes were glazed, his lids heavy.

"It is no trick," she whispered as the ripples of desire subsided. "I stole your memories when I stole your humanity. In seeking an explanation for what I did to you, you are seeking the truth. Whether you wish to accept it or not, you were a willing party in most things."

"No." His wide eyes were almost bulging out of their sockets. "I … I would have remembered."

"Your licentious conduct in the tavern marked you as someone deserving of a life of agonising torment," she said. "And I'm certain when you hear all I have to say you will not blame me for it. But if you want answers, you must accept that you were the one who made the ultimate decision."

"Decision," he repeated sounding somewhat delirious. "What decision?"

Ivana smiled. "You begged me to bite you, Leo."

CHAPTER 5

$\mathcal{L}$eo jumped out of the metal tub. "You're lying," he said, ignoring his state of undress as he strode over to the bed. "What man of sound mind would want to live a life like this?"

Her amused gaze drifted over him, lingering on his chest, falling to the place no decent woman would dare to look. Desire still simmered inside. He knew it would not take much for his lust for pleasure to overwhelm him.

How could this be?

He wanted to drive his sword into her heart, drive his cock deep into her core.

"That is the point, Leo," she said, unperturbed by his angry countenance as she stood to face him. "You were not of sound mind. You were possessed by a need for carnal pleasures. Indeed, your weakness for the sins of the flesh led me to you."

She was speaking, but he was struggling to listen.

Despite his ire, he could not shake the erotic images of their coupling she'd infused into his mind. They felt so real to him. The level of satisfaction he experienced at the moment of climax was like nothing he had ever felt with anyone else before.

Were they forgotten memories? Or was this just another form of cruel manipulation?

He was determined to find out.

"If what you say is true, if we were joined as you have shown me, then kiss me now. Let me feel the truth from your lips."

Fear flashed in her bright blue eyes, and she swallowed visibly. "I … I can't."

Anger pushed to the fore, anger mixed with an odd sense of disappointment. He knew his request would reveal her to be a liar. "What?" he mocked. "We shared one passionate night and now—"

"Six nights," she corrected.

Leo took a step back, her declaration dinting his usually impenetrable armour. Six nights? Two nights for every year as a monster was a heavy price to pay for pleasure.

"You kept me here for six nights?" he said incredulously. Six blasted nights and all he could recall was a flight of dusty stone steps.

"I did not keep you here." She glanced at the floor but noting his cock was but a few inches away from her gown, her gaze shot back to meet his. "Yes. I may have manipulated your thoughts initially. When I first brought you here, my intention was to hurt you as you hurt others, to make you pay for all eternity. But I made a mistake. I should have dealt with the matter elsewhere."

Leo recalled Elliot's recount of the night the golden-haired devil turned him. "You mean you should have abused me in the graveyard, left me on the cold floor of a mausoleum."

Her eyes grew wide, and she whispered, "You speak of Elliot?"

"Of course I speak of him. Why, have there been others?" The thought of an army of gentlemen imprisoned in tombs during daylight hours sent bolts of rage racing through him. He grabbed her by her upper arms and shook her. "How many more are there? How many? Tell me. How many men have you sunk your rotten teeth into?"

"Three," she gasped. "There have only been three."

At the sight of her fearful expression, something snapped inside him. He did not know why a sudden wave of sympathy swept over him or why the need to soothe her overtook all else. His gaze fell to her full lips, slightly parted as she panted for breath.

Hell and damnation!

It was like there were two men inside him—one eager for revenge, the other desperate to bed her, to love her again.

A solitary tear trickled down her cheek. "You loved me once," she whispered as though party to his thoughts. "You were kind and tender."

"I don't remember a blasted thing." He pulled her closer to his needy body as only one thought consumed him. "But I intend to rectify that problem."

Without another word, he claimed her lips. The kiss was rough, impatient, far from gentle. Within seconds, desire ignited in a powerful explosion of lust and longing. She clutched his shoulders; he gripped her soft buttocks as he rubbed against her. Their tongues became lost in each other's mouths, their groans and pants audible proof of their uncontrollable passion.

Bloody hell!

No other woman had ever tasted as good. A fire burned inside him, a desperate urge to pound into her over and over again. All other thoughts became incoherent amidst the voice telling him to take her—right now. As the need grew more intense, his fangs burst from their sheath. The sweet taste of her blood as the sharp points grazed the sensitive skin of her lips was like a potent aphrodisiac.

Damn. He was so hard he wanted to tear her gown from her luscious body, sink his teeth into her neck and drink the nectar of the gods.

Never in all his lascivious liaisons had he been able to express himself so freely. Even though he despised the monster within, the sheer strength emanating from him, the overwhelming sense of hunger tearing through his veins made the experience all the more pleasurable.

Was this what he had been searching for night after night when he wandered the ballrooms of the *ton*? Was the hope of rekindling a forgotten memory the real reason behind his constant search for satisfaction?

Elliot was right about his preoccupation with a particular type of female.

The thought of his friend and brother brought him crashing down from the dizzying heights of ecstasy. To bury himself deep inside this woman would mean betraying the brother who had saved him.

With a sense of deep anguish, he tore his mouth from hers and stared into the beguiling face responsible for his torment. The whites of her eyes were tinged red; her fangs were visible too.

"I ... I can't," he panted, though his body wanted nothing more than to mate with her. "I cannot betray the brotherhood."

She remained silent as she stared at him. Despite numerous efforts, he could not read her thoughts.

"You were right," he continued as he stepped back, shock

and a bittersweet craving ravaging his thoughts. His jutting erection proved too much of a distraction, and he moved to the bed, grabbed the breeches and dragged them up over his hips. "An undeniable connection exists between us. But I cannot forget the pain and misery you have caused, to me and to others."

She sighed, flopped down onto the bed as though her legs could no longer support her weight. "I understand. I knew what would happen once our lips met. Perhaps when you hear all I have to say you may think a little differently. Perhaps when I have explained why I let you go, you will know I am not the devil you believe me to be."

Curiosity flared.

"One thing is certain," he said, trying to sound amused as a way of easing the wave of sadness taking hold. "I no longer have need for my sword."

How could he take her head now?

She gave a weak smile as the white points disappeared and her eyes sparkled again. "Then I have accomplished something this evening." She stood, located her robe and shrugged her arms into it while he reached for the shirt and threw it over his head. "Come. Let us resume our conversation downstairs. In a place where we are not apt to give in to temptation."

"I'll need to drink." Nothing she could give him to soothe his craving would taste as good as her blood.

"Of course. Once we've spoken, it will be too late, too hazardous to attempt to return to the tavern before sunrise. I suggest you accept the offer of a bed and rest here until night falls again."

Leo considered the row of windows spanning the length of the room. "I assume you do not stay in here once the sun has come up?"

She shook her head. "No. I have a different chamber for the daylight hours. Some rooms here are accessible before dusk, but Sylvester will explain it to you when he escorts you to your room."

As they descended the narrow staircase, it occurred to him that he did not know her name. "Again, you seem to have an advantage," he said, feeling a little calmer, more relaxed in her company. "You know my name, yet I do not know yours."

"You have forgotten many things," she said as he suddenly pictured himself crying out her name in the wild throes of passion.

It came to him then as clear as the stars in a cloudless sky. "Ivana," he whispered. "It's Ivana."

She smiled, and the warm glow in his chest returned. "It sounds good to hear it fall from your lips again," she said as he followed her into the Great Hall.

With the vaulted ceiling towering fifty feet or more above, the arched beams were an impressive sight to behold. A huge stone hearth filled one wall; the giant trophy heads of numerous animals littered another. There were few windows. Had it not been for the bright orange flames burning in the grate, Leo imagined the room would feel dark and oppressive. It posed the perfect place for a creature of the night to relax during daylight hours.

"Please sit," she said, gesturing to the two chairs hugging the fire. "I keep but a small staff, for obvious reasons. Julia will attend to us this evening."

He understood the need for privacy. "With the nature of our affliction, there are not many people one can trust."

She nodded. "I would trust Julia and Sylvester with my life."

"Then you are truly blessed." His thoughts drifted back to Elliot and Alexander. He hoped they would understand his reasons for coming to Bavaria. Nevertheless, he had no idea how he would explain the recent turn of events.

Blood was brought to them in tall glass vials. Leo turned the thin cylindrical object around in his fingers before drinking down the rich burgundy liquid. He handed the empty tube back to a nervous-looking Julia, finding the process vastly different from the way he usually fed.

Elliot had taught him to find pleasure in the ritual. To drink as one would the finest wine or cognac. Ivana's method lent itself more to the medicinal: a foul tincture to be drunk quickly, neatly, the used vessel removed so as not to remind the patient of their dreadful condition.

"Am I to assume you do not take pleasure in drinking?" Leo asked, curious to know the reason behind her detached approach.

Ivana glanced at the opening of his shirt, moistened her lips when her gaze drifted up to his neck. "I have on occasion. But it is like drinking vinegar as opposed to … well, I am not sure you would understand."

The vial had contained goat's blood. His experienced palate could identify the animal purely from the taste. But she was mistaken if she believed him immune to the potent lure of drinking directly from the host.

"I have drunk from the source," he said, for once feeling no shame for admitting the truth. "Numerous times."

Her eyes grew large as she sat forward. "But you can't … you mustn't. Yes, perhaps only the first time when your body is embracing the change. But I manipulated your thoughts so you would not hurt others anymore."

"Then in my case you have failed." He steepled his fingers as he examined the frown marring her brow. "I have drunk from the pretty necks of a few women."

Indeed, in those moments, it was like another man

possessed his mind and body. In those moments when he lost control, Elliot was always there to take care of things.

Ivana's hand shot up to her throat. "You drank directly from a vein?" she muttered almost to herself as she shook her head so vigorously one could not mistake the fact she found the idea abhorrent. "Leo, you must not do so again. Promise me. Promise me you won't."

Anger flared in his chest. He would not be drinking blood at all had it not been for the night she sank her fangs into his neck. Why should she be concerned for him now?

"I've spent the last three years fighting the urge to bite. Sometimes, I am just too weak to resist."

"But you must. You do not understand—"

"It seems there are many things I don't understand," he interjected with an air of frustration. "Many things I don't remember."

She came down to kneel on the floor in front of him and put her hands on his knees. His cock stirred as he conjured an image of her taking him into her mouth.

Bloody hell!

The animalistic instincts he always fought against were so prominent, so powerful when in her presence. The desperate urge to mate with her, to drink from her, to have her completely at his mercy was compelling.

"It is my fault, Leo. When we were joined, we … we drank from each other. It heightened our pleasure, made us stronger, made us feel invincible."

They had bitten each other whilst he'd thrust inside her?

The erotic image played out before his eyes. Hell, no wonder he struggled to control the devil inside when parading about the ballrooms of Mayfair.

Come to think of it, every woman he had ever bitten had possessed blue eyes and golden hair. Elliot often mocked him for it. Relief coursed through him. He had always thought himself to be the weakest brother, the most infantile, the most reckless. Now it seemed he had been desperately trying to recapture a memory.

"It all makes more sense to me now," he said, staring meditatively into the flames. He was silent while his mind absorbed all she had said. When his gaze locked with hers, he could see the truth in her eyes. "I've spent the last three years looking for *you*. I've spent three years searching for the same level of satisfaction I must have experienced here."

His words did not placate her. "Drinking from the source alters you. It hardens your heart to all emotion. It makes you see things differently." She glanced down, struggled to look him in the eye. "It is part of the reason I let you go."

Her voice broke on the last word, the high-pitched cry revealing suppressed emotion. She shot to her feet and turned away from him to gaze into the flames.

Leo stood and put his hand on her shoulder. "What do you mean, Ivana, when you say you let me go?"

She turned to face him, her eyes red and watery. Never in his wildest imagination would he have believed the devil woman capable of shedding a tear.

"There is so much to tell you," she whispered as he wiped a tear away with the pad of this thumb. "So much I have kept hidden inside."

"Then you must tell me everything. That's the reason I came here, to understand why you chose to punish us."

"And to seek revenge," she added.

"Yes, that too. But things are different now. I painted a picture in my mind, and I have lived in constant fear of the image. Now, in reality, the scene is not how I remember it. The lines are distorted, the figures hazy. What appeared grotesque no longer rouses the same feelings of disdain within me."

"Then let us sit, let me paint a different picture for you. Let me settle your mind before you leave here."

The thought of leaving caused a sudden stabbing pain in his chest. In truth, he had never felt at home anywhere. In the ballrooms of London, he could not be himself; he was just another actor playing a role, just another gentleman looking for a way to fill his time. Life held no meaning. Without his friends, his brothers, he had nothing.

Yet here, in the darkest depths of the devil woman's lair, he felt normal.

He felt as though he belonged.

CHAPTER 6

*T*he taste of Leo's lips had been her undoing.

During the journey in the carriage, she imagined giving him the explanation he desired. Hoping then he would leave satisfied in the knowledge she'd had a justifiable reason for turning him. Either that or he would use his sword to put her out of her misery for good.

But as soon as he stepped over the threshold, memories of their time together in the castle came flooding back and her steely composure crumbled. Since that first night, there had been an unexplainable attraction between them. The feeling went deeper than lust, perhaps even deeper than love—if there was such an emotion.

The years since their separation had been unbearable. Her bleeding heart had not even begun to heal. She could find no logic or reason for the depth of feeling consuming her. The number of nights or the length of time spent in his company held no significance. An hour spent together was as fulfilling as an entire lifetime for others.

"Start at the beginning," Leo said, settling back into his

chair and crossing his legs at his ankles. He looked relaxed, comfortable, but would not remain so for long.

"Then I shall begin with the night I bit the lord in the mausoleum," she said wearily. She could not bear to talk of the night she lost her own humanity. "I was bitter, resentful, consumed by anger. I had been watching him for days, witnessed various unscrupulous acts."

"You speak of Elliot. He has a name, Ivana." She could hear the hint of contempt in his tone. "You should know that both Elliot and Alexander are like brothers to me."

She should have been surprised, but with their thoughts aligned and their powers for mind manipulation, she supposed it was inevitable they would find one another. "You were drawn to those who share an affinity for blood. The bonds formed during times of adversity are not easily broken."

"Without Elliot's friendship, I would not be sitting here. Was he the first person you turned?"

An image of her sinking her fangs into Nikolai's foul neck flashed into her mind, and she shuddered, repulsed she should even think of it after all this time. "Yes. Elliot was the first man I poisoned with my tainted blood."

Leo suddenly straightened, banged his fist on the arm of the chair. "God damn it, why?"

"Because of the children," she implored. She would do anything to protect them, to save them from pain. She threw her hands in the air. "It is all for the children."

Leo shook his head, confusion marring his brow. "But I don't understand how the two are connected."

Ivana took a deep breath as she would need to remain calm if she had any hope of finishing this tale.

"Herr Bruhn takes care of the children, the illegitimate offspring of the fine lords who pass through here and the servant women who will do anything to put food on the table." Just saying the words aloud caused resentment to flare. "They come with their lofty manners and deceitful words, take their pleasure and leave nothing but misery behind in their wake. Poor innocent souls are discarded as though they are nothing, and it tears at my heart, rips it to shreds."

He sat in silence. She watched him swallow visibly as his gaze focused on a point of no interest on the floor.

"Some women travel from the nearest town," she continued, desperate to make him understand. "Some are lured away by the promise of trinkets and pretty baubles. They leave the child of one gentleman behind when they go off with another. Some are not as lucky." She swallowed, moistened her lips. "I do not blame the women. I blame the men desperate to satisfy their needs regardless of the human cost. Those men do not deserve the precious gift of life."

Indeed, she blamed Nicolai, too. For taking a sweet, naive girl and turning her into a freak of nature, a monster left all alone, abandoned to the night.

Leo swallowed and then asked with an incredulous expression, "Is that why you turned Elliot, because of his licentious ways?"

Ivana sneered. "You should have seen him and his blatant disregard for others. If you would only come to see the children, Leo, you would know why I was forced to stop him. Now he can satisfy his needs without spreading his seed. Now he cannot hide the monster beneath his elegant clothes and fancy words. Now he must spend eternity in the knowledge he will never find someone who will accept him when they see him for what he truly is."

"You're wrong," he snorted. "Elliot has recently married.

His wife knows of his affliction, has witnessed him change. They are deeply in love."

Ivana gasped in shock, but then upon reflection said, "Then I expect he will want to thank me. The man I met in the mausoleum was incapable of expressing any genuine emotion."

Leo stood and walked over to the fire, placed his hands flat on the stone over-mantel as his head fell forward.

She could hear his muttered curses, sense his inner torment, feel his confusion and pain. He picked up the poker and stabbed at the glowing embers as though they had wronged him in some way.

"Did you take Elliot as your lover, too?" He did not turn to face her. "Did you lie with him like you did me?"

Ivana shot up and put her hand on his shoulder. "Good Lord, no." If only Leo could remember what he meant to her. If only he could remember all they had shared, then he would not have asked such a ridiculous question.

He shrugged her hand away, but she remained at his shoulder. "And what of Alexander? He told me you brought him here in your carriage. He recalled lying on your bed."

"And did he tell you what he was doing when I lured him away from the tavern? Did he?"

"No."

"Then you should know I have never met a gentleman so open in his vulgarity. It took every effort not to drain him dry where he sat."

"Yet still you brought him to your home." He dropped the poker and turned to face her. She could see the disappointment in his eyes. "If he disgusted you as you say, why bring him here?"

The sudden pain in her chest caused her throat to constrict, and she fought back the flurry of emotion. "I brought him here because of you," she cried. "I thought I could use him to forget you. I thought having him here would help to eradicate your memory. But I should have known it was an impossible task."

"How long did he stay?"

"Two hours."

Leo jerked his head back, and his disapproving stare cut her to the bone. "So you bit him and discarded him without a second thought?"

Ivana nodded as she gazed at the floor. "I couldn't bear to have him here. Sylvester took him to the forest and left him there."

He took a step towards her. "Did you not consider the fact he might be scared, terrified at the thought of waking to find he craved blood?"

"Did he consider the fact he could have fathered a child? That the child would be abandoned, left frightened and all alone with no way to fend for itself?"

Leo exhaled loudly but did not answer her question. "You said you had only turned three men. So there has been no one else since Alexander?"

"No."

"Why?"

Because now I know I could not bear to touch another man, to drink from him, share my blood so intimately with him.

"I … I found another way to be rid of them," she said. "It takes but a drop of my blood in their ale for me to command their thoughts. It is far easier when they are inebriated to manipulate their minds."

He snorted. "I suppose I should be relieved that there are not more men with our affliction."

She could feel him withdrawing, pulling away from her, putting up a barrier.

"Come with me tomorrow," she pleaded. "I will be calling on Herr Bruhn as I do most nights. Come see the children and then you will understand my motives."

He dropped into the chair, his weary sigh tearing at her heart. "I do not know what to make of it all," he said, pushing his hands through his hair. "I do not know what to think."

"You do not need to think anything. Take some time. Meet the children." She sounded desperate for his approval, although after what she had done, she would never receive it. "But you should rest now."

She would not rest tonight. She would lie in her bed trying hard not to think of him, of his kiss, his touch, of the way he'd once loved her.

"What of me?" he muttered. "You must have been watching me too. You must have disapproved of my antics. You brought me here in your carriage, forced me to sleep."

"You were drunk, behaving recklessly. When you took—" She closed her eyes briefly, swallowed down the pain the memory evoked. "When you took the maid from the tavern to your bed, I knew then it would only be a matter of time before you fathered a child here."

"I understand that now, Ivana. I understand why you lured me from the tavern. I recall following you up through the forest until you bundled me into your carriage. Although, at the time, I didn't know you sought to rob me of my humanity. But I still don't understand why you brought me here."

It had not been her intention, but some things were destined to be. "Do you believe in fate, Leo? Do you believe we will recognise our predetermined path if we look for the signs, the markers?"

"If I didn't, I do now," he said with a shrug.

"I dreamt of you, many times. I did not know it was you until we were in my carriage and something forced me to taste your lips while you were sleeping." Her heart skipped a beat as the vision flooded her mind. "That was all it took. Just one kiss and I knew I had found you."

He thrust forward, hit his chest numerous times with his clenched fist. "Yet still you turned me into this."

"As I said, you wanted to be with me. You felt the connection too. You wanted us to be together always. You might say a person could not possibly express such a depth of emotion after only a few short days. But I say, when you find the one you have lived with through many lifetimes, mortal time has no meaning, no value, no measure."

"If I felt that way, why would I leave?"

"Because I did not give you a choice."

Because he meant too much to her. Because to let him stay would have meant risking everything.

"It is the reason I have not helped you to remember all that happened here," she said with some reluctance. "It is the reason I cannot allow you to stay now."

"You want me to leave?" he said, his tone revealing his shock.

"No. I have never wanted that. But I don't want you to die. I don't want to leave Herr Bruhn with no means to provide for the children. I don't want to put their lives in danger, make them targets for someone who would want to use them to hurt me."

His eyes widened. "I can speak for both Elliot and Alexander when I say we would never use innocent children to hurt you."

He did not understand. Only one person had the power to ruin everything. Only one person could take away all the things that meant so much to her. The longer Leo stayed at the castle, the greater the chance she would take him to her bed. In that moment of wild, reckless abandonment, her heart would be open, her thoughts transported freely to the one person she desperately wanted to keep in the dark.

"Then I thank you for putting my mind at ease," she said to placate him.

Leo sighed. "There is still one more thing I'm struggling to understand."

"What is that?"

There were many secrets he had no knowledge of.

He rubbed his chin as he narrowed his gaze. "You were prepared to die tonight. You stood with your arms raised to the heavens and waited for me to end it all. Why?"

It was never her life she feared for.

"Because we are living a nightmare. Because I have experienced paradise, cleansed my soul in its crystal clear waters, felt the brilliant rays of happiness warm my skin." She closed her eyes and imagined feeling the glorious moment again. But her world was dark, bleak, hopeless. "When you have lost something so precious, life has little meaning."

"What of the children?"

"I shall always provide for their material needs. But one day, I must leave them. They can never know what I am. As they grow, it will become more difficult for me to maintain a relationship with them. To lose someone through death is perhaps easier than to be abandoned by them."

"I understand what it's like to feel alone," he said. "But do not underestimate the devastation caused when someone dies. I am living proof it alters people, moulds them into a person they might never have become if not for the loss. Yet for those who are forsaken, there is always hope."

She gave a weak smile. "Then I should be thankful your

desire for answers was more important to you than your desire for revenge."

All this talk of death and loneliness made her feel tired, weary. She needed to quench her sudden thirst and the magnificent man before her always proved too tempting to resist.

"I must retire now." She stood, and he did too. "Sylvester will escort you to your chamber. Will you come with me to visit the children tomorrow or are we to part for good this night?"

The raw emotion flashing in his eyes pained her. Oh, how she wanted to soothe his soul. How she wanted to show him the beauty to be found in their joining.

"I will come to see the children. I would know everything before I return to England."

An icy chill penetrated her bones.

To tell him everything would inevitably bring the Devil to her door.

CHAPTER 7

*H*err Bruhn welcomed them into his home. A look of relief, and then suspicion, marred his heavily lined brow. Leo smiled in the hope it would reassure him. After witnessing Leo wielding his sword, he did not blame the man for being wary.

"It is good to see you, Frau Lockwood," Herr Bruhn said, clasping the lady's gloved hand.

Frau Lockwood, not Fraulein?

Leo wondered why the old man had used the title. It never occurred to him Ivana could be widowed. A wave of jealousy surged through his body at the thought she had loved a man enough to marry him. Or perhaps it was simply a case of her wishing to appear less vulnerable. Such stunning features would surely attract a gentleman's eye, although woe betide any man who sought to take advantage.

The old man's gaze flitted back and forth between them.

"You remember the gentleman who helped me home last night?" she said, putting a hand on Leo's arm. The affectionate gesture was given purely to placate Herr Bruhn's fears, but her touch sparked the usual warm feeling of familiarity.

"Yes, yes," Herr Bruhn nodded as he turned his attention to Leo. "I am pleased to see you have left that sword of yours at home. I fear it would frighten the children."

Ivana smiled. "Leo is often over-cautious. But perhaps the children might like to see a genuine knight going about his duties."

She had introduced him in a tone and manner befitting a servant. He suppressed the need to correct her, to offer a bow and boast of his ancestral roots. When possessed with their deviant affliction, it would not be wise to draw undue attention.

"Welcome, welcome." Herr Bruhn gestured for them to enter the parlour. The tempting smell of freshly baked bread wafted through the house. "Have you both eaten?"

Ivana nodded. "Yes, we dined before we left. I am ashamed to admit we were rather ravenous and couldn't possibly eat another thing."

"Ah, never mind," Herr Bruhn said with a hint of disappointment. "The children have made bread, and I know how they like to please you."

Leo pulled Ivana's cape from her shoulders, pleased to hear her sharp intake of breath when his fingers brushed against the soft skin at her nape. "Frau Lockwood has eaten far too much this evening, but I will happily try the bread if you think the children will not object."

With its dry, clumpy texture, he found bread hard to swallow, but Elliot had taught him to tolerate small quantities of food and drink.

A brief look of panic flashed in Ivana's blue eyes. "Are you sure you can manage to eat anything more?"

Leo gave an arrogant smirk. "A piece of bread won't make much difference."

"Excellent." Herr Bruhn clapped his hands but then his expression grew solemn as he turned to Ivana. "I thought you did not look well when you left here last night. Your face held an almost deathly pallor, and the damp air will only make matters worse. You should not have ventured out this evening."

Leo felt a tinge of guilt. She had sensed his presence, had expected to meet her demise. Despite everything she'd said about being prepared to die, the ashen complexion Herr Bruhn noted would surely have been attributed to fear.

"I am fine now I have eaten," she reassured. "And you know there is nothing that would prevent me from visiting the children."

Herr Bruhn turned to him. "She is an angel sent from the Lord."

Ivana's cheeks flushed berry red, and she looked to the floor.

"Do not be modest," the old man continued. "Without you, where would these poor children be?"

For once in his miserable existence, Leo was left dumb-struck. During all of his licentious encounters, the thought of fathering offspring had never really concerned him. Yes, at times he had sheathed his manhood as a means of warding off infection. He had mastered the art of withdrawal, knew that some women soaked sponges with anything acidic enough to act as a deadly barrier.

What had once seemed like the irresponsible pursuits of an aristocratic gentleman, now felt like the vulgar actions of a scoundrel.

"Come, come through to the fire," Herr Bruhn continued.

Ivana glanced at him as they followed the old man into

the parlour. "You see. Not everyone believes I am a cold-hearted devil," she whispered.

"Evidently, you're loved and well-respected here."

"Please sit." Herr Bruhn gestured to the two chairs hugging the hearth. "I shall go and find the children."

Leo watched him scuttle out. "How many children live here?" He glanced around the room smaller than the cupboard he reserved for his boots.

"Five," Ivana replied from the seat opposite. "Matilda is the eldest and will be ten next month. Christoph is three and the youngest here."

A sudden wave of panic passed over him. It had been three years since he'd visited the village.

"Christoph is not your son, if that is what's worrying you," she said, reading his thoughts. "He will be four next week."

She gave a weak smile upon hearing his audible sigh of relief. While some men were preoccupied with furthering their bloodline, Leo had never wanted to be a father. Indeed, Elliot would probably argue that he couldn't even look after himself. But it had more to do with seeing his father die at such a young age. The responsibility of a marquessate proved too much for him, his heart too weak to withstand the burden.

"You can't blame me for thinking the worst," he said.

"Frau Lockwood. Frau Lockwood."

Two boys ran into the parlour, and he recognised them as the ones she had chastised the night before. They stood to attention before her as though she was a naval captain and they were lowly cabin hands desperate to make a good impression.

"What have I said about running?" Herr Bruhn hurried in behind them, carrying a small boy who appeared rather sleepy. "If you trip over the rug, you're sure to lose your teeth."

Two girls entered the room; the younger one carried a tray while the older girl guided her to the small table. "We've been baking bread," the younger girl said, her excited eyes twinkling.

Ivana smiled. "And it looks wonderful, Martha."

Despite Ivana's cheerful countenance, Leo could sense her anxiety. She could not eat the bread.

"It smells delicious, too," he added. "I can hardly wait to try some."

After introducing herself as Matilda, the older girl cut a slice, buttered the surface with care and handed it to him.

"A plate, you need a plate," Herr Bruhn said in a mild state of panic as he put the younger boy, Christoph, down.

Matilda jumped and almost sent the tray crashing to the floor.

"It doesn't matter about the crockery," Leo said, taking a bite of the bread.

Ivana sucked in a breath as her fearful gaze bore into him.

The bread was moist and being freshly baked was consequently easier to swallow than Leo had anticipated. His stomach did spasm once or twice, but he managed to finish it without gagging.

"It was delicious," he said, and they all cheered for him as they had done for Ivana when she'd nibbled on the sweet biscuit.

Ivana's shocked expression was quickly replaced with one of utter joy. The muscles in his abdomen grew taut as his desire for her flared. He would eat a whole loaf just to witness such a breathtaking sight, just to see a smile touch her lips.

"Would you care for something to wash it down?" Herr

Bruhn asked, appearing a little more relaxed in Leo's company.

"What do you have?"

Herr Bruhn's eyes lit up. "I have a new beer. It is clearer, not as murky as the ale they serve in the tavern."

"Very well," he nodded, "But just a small mug as I must see Frau Lockwood safely home."

"Of course, of course," he said, nodding to himself as he rushed off.

For a moment, the room fell silent. They stared at each other, oblivious to the children's gapes. Leo felt her gratitude explode in his chest, mingled with something else, perhaps respect, perhaps something more undefinable.

"Would you care to try the bread, Frau Lockwood?"

Ivana turned to look at Matilda's eager face. "Could I take mine home with me?"

"You'd best hurry and wrap it up," Leo said in an attempt to ease the girl's disappointment. "Else I might end up eating it all."

Matilda laughed, as did Ivana and then all the children chuckled.

Christoph came up to him and held his hands up. Leo was forced to swallow the hard lump forming in his throat. No one had ever looked at him with such admiration. He was used to fake compliments, feigned interest, had never witnessed a look so genuine.

"He wants you to pick him up," Ivana said. "He does not say very much, the odd word now and then, but we are helping him with his speech."

The boy smiled, and the familiarity of his countenance hit Leo like a hard punch to his gut. He had only ever seen eyes as green once before. He recognised the amber flecks, the hair as dark as ebony. He gulped a breath as his frantic gaze shot to Ivana.

She nodded in response. "It is as you suspect."

Bloody hell!

Elliot had a child and knew nothing of it.

Feeling an overwhelming need to offer comfort, he picked the boy up, hugged him tight to his chest. Hell, the surge of emotion almost choked him; his hands were shaking, his thoughts in complete disarray.

"You've always known?" he asked as Ivana dabbed at the corner of her eye.

"Yes."

Damn it all. Despite her feelings of disdain for Elliot, she had cared for his son as her own. He didn't know how to feel. Anger flowed through him. He was angry with himself for being so negligent, so blind to the realities of life. He was angry with Elliot for the same reason. His heart ached for his friend and brother, who knew nothing of the beautiful boy he had left behind. Christ, he could feel tears welling in his eyes and he kissed the boy on the top of his head for fear he'd turn into a blubbering wreck.

What the hell was he to do now?

The boy held his palms together and opened them back and forth.

"He wants you to read to him tonight." Ivana's voice quivered as she spoke. "But don't feel you have to. I'm more than happy to read to them."

Leo gazed up at the sea of desperate faces, all nodding at him as their eyes grew wide. "Of course I'll read to them if they would like me to."

One of the older boys stepped forward. "We would, we would."

Herr Bruhn returned with two tankards of beer. The old

man watched him sip his drink, gave a shriek of delight when Leo expressed his approval. Despite the sadness consuming him over recent revelations, Leo was amused by Ivana's baffled expression every time he swallowed a mouthful.

Ivana led him up to the children's bedchamber. The girls shared one room, the three boys another, but they all piled in together to hear Leo tell his tale. It hadn't occurred to him that the book would not be written in English and Ivana helped him read *Der Froschkönig oder der eiserne Heinrich - The Frog King or Iron Henry.*

It wasn't reading the tale of the spoilt princess or the frog prince that resonated with him, but the plight of the servant with three irons bands surrounding his heart to prevent it from breaking when he learns of his master's curse. Indeed, when Leo gazed into Christoph's bright green eyes, he wished such a thing were possible.

As he tucked the boys into their beds one thing became abundantly clear. Meeting the children had altered him, changed him in some inexplicable way. Anger still simmered beneath the surface. To the point where he believed he could quite easily rip the throats from every noble scoundrel gracing the ballrooms of the *ton*.

He was standing over Christoph when Ivana touched him on the arm. "We should be going now," she whispered.

Leo turned to face the woman he had spent years despising, years blaming for ruining their lives when they had done an excellent job of doing so themselves. His heart swelled with a desperate need to repay her for her kindness to Elliot's son.

Hell, his mind was a jumbled mess of contradictions.

She moved her hand to his shoulder, and he felt an overwhelming urge to make her happy. Indeed, as his cock stirred, there was nothing jumbled or confusing about the desire thrumming through his veins.

"Then we will say goodnight to Herr Bruhn and be on our way." He followed her from the room, stopping in the doorway to take another look at the boy he would regard as his nephew from now on. "Will we come here again tomorrow?" he asked.

"I put the children to bed most nights. It gives Herr Bruhn an extra hour to himself. His wife is ill, and it has been difficult for him these past two weeks."

The nature of their affliction meant they could not visit during the day, and he sensed Ivana's frustration at being unable to do more.

"They will all be asleep soon," she said as Herr Bruhn met them at the bottom of the stairs.

"Excellent." He clapped his hands. "Frau Bruhn is awake and has asked to see you. Just for a minute or two before you leave. I will keep your friend company."

Ivana nodded. "Of course. I am relieved she has regained some strength." She touched Leo on the arm again. "I will be but a moment."

As soon as she left them, Herr Bruhn led him into the parlour. "I must speak with you before Frau Lockwood returns," he whispered, his frantic gaze glancing over Leo's shoulder. "I am so worried about her."

"What is it?" Leo's heart was beating so fast he feared it would jump from his throat. "Is there something wrong with her?"

"I fear she worries too much, about me, about the children. It is making her ill. She comes here night after night and never eats or drinks a thing." Herr Bruhn sucked in a breath before continuing in the same rushed manner. "And she looks so sad, so pale. I wonder if it's because she does not wish to take food from the children's mouths. But she is so generous with her time and money I do not want her to worry about us."

"She cares greatly for the children," Leo said with a sigh. So much so, she had committed abhorrent acts to prevent any more little ones from perishing. "But rest assured, I have sat with her while she has taken nourishment. During my stay, I shall ensure her needs are taken care of. I promise you that."

Leo had planned to stay at the castle for an hour, which had soon turned into the night. Now, everything had changed. Ivana expected him to leave, but he would stay to be near Christoph until he decided what to do. He would stay to be near Ivana. Despite having no memory of the event, remnants of a long-lost love, of a painful separation, lingered deep within him.

Herr Bruhn grasped his upper arm. "That is what I hoped you would say. You must take care of her. She is very precious to us."

"I understand perfectly," he said, the need to protect her pushing to the fore.

The more time he spent in her company, the more his need for her grew. Never had he cared so deeply for a woman. The more he thought of it, the more he knew there was only one path to take, only one course of action on this road of discovery. He would join with her as he had before. He would know the true depth of their passion. He would do everything in his power to remember what it was like to love her.

CHAPTER 8

*I*vana smiled at Herr Bruhn as he closed the door behind them, but in truth, she struggled to fight back the tears. Frau Bruhn had held her hand, muttered a few words, but appeared too weak and pale, so close to—

"Is everything all right?" Leo's question permeated her sorrowful musings. "You're not the same since you went to speak to Frau Bruhn."

Ivana gave a hopeless sigh and shook her head as they walked back to her carriage. "I'm afraid, Leo. I'm afraid Frau Bruhn won't recover from her illness. I'm afraid it will all be too much for Herr Bruhn to cope with. I don't know what will happen to the children. I don't know what more I can do to help them."

She saw pity in his eyes when she met his gaze.

"I'll be honest with you," Leo said, and she could sense a slight reluctance to speak. "Perhaps it is time to find them homes elsewhere. The Bruhns are elderly and cannot care for the children indefinitely." He paused briefly. "When, or if, I return to England, I want to take Christoph with me."

Panic flared.

How could she tear Christoph away from the only family he had ever known? The other boys would miss him terribly. And how would she cope when the time came for Leo to leave again?

"Take him away?" She almost choked on the words. But she knew that the boy's time with the Bruhns would soon come to an end if Frau Bruhn took a turn for the worse. "Do you think Elliot would welcome the boy?"

Leo shrugged. "I have no idea. But I would like to think so. Granted, the nature of our affliction would make it much more difficult for him to care for a child. The fact his wife is unaffected would make the task easier."

Ivana could not imagine his wife would be happy at the prospect of raising another woman's son, particularly when it was impossible for her to conceive.

"Does his wife know he cannot give her a child of her own?"

"She knows everything," Leo nodded. "They have no secrets."

Guilt surfaced as she heard his mild reproof. A relationship based on love, mutual respect, honesty, and trust was what she had always longed for. But life's complications had made such a dream impossible.

"Then you believe she will openly accept another woman's child to please her husband?"

"Grace is a good, kind person who has saved my friend and brother from a miserable existence. I'm certain her heart is big enough to push aside any doubts or fears she may have."

"Under other circumstances, I would have liked to meet her," Ivana said. "But no doubt she would wish to drive a stake through my heart for what I have done to her beloved husband."

"I'm certain, once she met the children, she would understand your motives." He held the carriage door open for her. "Even if they are somewhat extreme."

"And what of you, Leo? How do you feel now you have met the children?"

"I feel as though I have spent many years walking about with my eyes closed." He spoke softly. "Now I can see why you would be angry and hurt at the prospect of them being left alone."

She stared into his warm brown eyes, recalling how his heated gaze was able to penetrate her soul during their intense coupling. "It means a lot that you understand why I behaved as I did. It is good to know you do not despise me as you once did."

She climbed into her conveyance. Leo followed her, falling into the seat opposite as the carriage pulled away and rattled along the cobbled street.

"It's fair to say I have a better grasp of the situation than I did a few days ago," he said as he studied her. "Indeed, I am curious to know more about my time here."

Despite the turbulent rocking, she sat forward, put her hand on his knee and the muscles flexed beneath her fingers. "Let us talk of the past no more. Know that everything I have done has been out of love, even when my actions appear to be misguided."

"Love for whom, Ivana?" His tone sounded smooth, rich, like a lover's soft caress and he glanced down at her hand. "Just for the children?"

Ivana sat back. "No … yes. You know what the children mean to me." To declare her love for him so openly would be a mistake.

"Always so guarded," he mocked. "You may struggle to

speak the truth, but I can read it in your eyes, feel it in your tender touch."

"I have never denied my feelings for you," she managed to say, although she had made him forget what he meant to her.

The corners of his mouth curled up into a wicked grin as his brown eyes twinkled. "In the castle, you said that once our lips met, you knew I was the one you'd been dreaming of."

She swallowed deeply, wondering at his motive for making the comment. "Yes."

"I find it hard to believe it would take but a single kiss. I think you should show me what happened while I slept. Show me how one touch could rouse such a powerful emotion."

"You know I cannot do that." She shook her head vigorously as a way of convincing herself such an act was sheer folly.

"Then you leave me no choice but to use my imagination."

Leo stretched his arms out across the back of the leather seat and closed his eyes. Ivana heard his slow, rhythmical breathing, watched the rise and fall of his chest with interest. Seconds passed before she felt the warm sensation flare deep in her core. The sudden pulsing between her legs sent a bolt of desire racing through her body, forcing her to suck in a breath.

The fragments of memories flashing through her mind evoked the kiss they had shared in her chamber. Leo had an extraordinary ability to fuse his thoughts with hers. So much so, she knew if she closed her eyes she would believe she was still encompassed in his warm embrace.

When it came to the only man she had ever loved, she was weak and powerless to refuse him whatever his heart desired.

Just to torment her, he whispered, "I know you want me, Ivana. I know you are just as keen as I to relive the experience."

A desperate urge to surrender took hold, forcing her to make an error. Carried away on the blissful wave of ecstasy rippling through her, she closed her eyes. An erotic image of his naked body flooded her vision. She saw the joy on his face as he found his release inside her. She felt the inner peace that only enveloped her when she was with him.

"I want you so much it is killing me." The tremor in her voice mimicked the tumultuous beats of her heart.

She could not say no to him.

The fear that usually permeated her thoughts had been suppressed by her overwhelming need to join with her one true mate. If they were quick, if they remained enclosed in the carriage, then perhaps she could contain her emotion. Perhaps then no one else would learn of it.

He must have felt her resolve melting under the heat raging within.

"Come to me, Ivana. Let us indulge our desires."

Her eyes sprung open. She met his intense gaze and without another word flew to the opposite side of the carriage into his open arms.

Perhaps it was her need to hurry that made her tear at his clothes like a woman possessed. Perhaps it was the need to experience that which she had denied herself for so long that caused her to devour his mouth, as though she would die if she did not taste him again.

"Show me what I mean to you," he panted hoarsely. "Take me into your body." The urgency in his voice was unmistakable, and he unbuttoned his breeches to let his manhood spring free.

Ivana bunched her dress up to her waist to straddle him.

Ripples of pure ecstasy travelled through her as she slid slowly down on the solid length. Despite the slight resistance, her body having been starved of him for far too long, he impaled her with a loud roar of satisfaction.

"Oh, Leo," she gulped as she took him deep inside, gripped him tight as he filled her full. The sensation of partnering him in the most intimate of acts brought tears of pure joy to her eyes.

His hands were everywhere all at once: on her bare thighs, cupping her buttocks as he thrust quick and hard.

"Don't stop," she whispered, as he pounded into her over and over. Once would never be enough for her. She would rather die than be without him again. "Don't ever stop loving me."

"Bloody hell, I can't get enough of you," he growled before claiming her mouth, tasting her until their tongues became lost amidst the wild frenzy of moans and groans.

"It has been so long," she murmured as he moved to nip the sensitive skin on her neck. "I need you, Leo. For now, for always."

"I can't touch you like this. Turn around," he commanded, and she felt empty as he withdrew from her hungry body. "Kneel on the seat."

She did as he asked. Once under his spell, she would do anything he asked.

With one hand braced against the seat, the other holding her crumpled dress up around her waist, he came behind her and entered her in one long delicious slide.

"I want to hear you cry with pleasure," he said as he bent over her and his fingers found the sensitive spot begging for his touch.

"Oh, Leo," she moaned as he claimed her body. Her legs were trembling, yet her soul soared.

"You're mine, Ivana," he said as he drove deeper, as his fingers strummed a rhythm unique only to them. "Don't ever forget it. Don't ever deny me your love."

Ivana pushed hard against him in a bid to hurry, the audible slapping proof of the desperate need to find her release. The intense flames of passion spread to her heart. Each hot, wet plunge of his throbbing manhood roused a soft sigh.

"Don't leave me." The honest words fell unwittingly from her lips as her world exploded around him. Every part of her held him close. The muscles in her core gripped him tight; the muscle that was her heart swelled with undeniable love.

His groan of satisfaction was a sweet melody to her ears. "Lord, help me. You were right," he panted as his hands clutched her hips whilst he was still buried deep. "Everything about this feels right. We were meant to be together."

A tear trickled down her cheek, and she was thankful he could not see it. It was a tear to express her happiness at having had one more chance to love him. It was a tear to express her fear of the deadly power she knew their love would evoke.

"Forgive me," he said as he withdrew from her body.

Ivana suppressed a whimper. "What is there to forgive?" she said, straightening her dress as she turned and flopped down into the seat.

"For being too desperate to wait." He did not bother to cover himself, and she fought the urge to taste him in the intimate way he liked. "For not expressing the depth of my feelings."

"It is how things are with us," she said, thankful he had conveyed nothing other than lust. It was those powerful ripples of emotion that drifted through the night air, drawn to devious hearts and minds.

He smiled. "You're not curious to know how I feel?"

"I do not need to hear the words, Leo. I see it in your eyes. I feel it in your touch. Indeed, you have opened yourself to me already. It is just that you do not remember."

"Perhaps I'm glad I have no recollection of it," he said with a shrug before tucking the most tempting part of his anatomy back into his breeches. "I am enjoying this road to enlightenment immensely."

You will not feel the same when we reach our final destination.

"Indeed, I think we should spend the rest of the evening in your chamber," he continued. "I think I would like to take things a little slower, savour every single moment."

Ivana knew what would happen if they indulged themselves completely.

"We can't, Leo. We will drink from each other. It will be utter madness to risk everything, to hope that lust, love or whatever this is between us will be enough to banish the demons from our door."

"I am known for being reckless, Ivana. Until now, my life has held little meaning. I have never had a purpose. Let me stay here with you. Let me help you with the children. And each night I shall bury myself deep inside the only place I belong."

He was offering her the world, the only thing she had ever wanted.

And by God, she was tempted.

She looked into his eyes, looked through the mirror to the soul she had already spent an eternity loving.

"How adept are you with your sword?" she asked, as she considered surrendering to the light.

He raised a confident brow. "My tutor believed me to be exceptional. I have yet to meet a man equally matched."

"And how far are you willing to go to protect what we have?"

Leo narrowed his gaze, fell silent while he contemplated her question. "Nothing will stop me from having you, Ivana. Nothing will stop me from discovering all we could be to one another."

"Very well." She sighed. She could not fight her feelings for him anymore. "When we return to the castle, we will discuss alternative plans for the children. You must write to Elliot and tell him about Christoph, make sure your affairs are in order. I shall speak to Herr Bruhn. And may I suggest you keep your sword close, preferably next to my bed."

CHAPTER 9

"*L*ook at them," Alexander whispered through gritted teeth. They stood at the tavern bar observing their wives sitting at the crude wooden table. "Anyone would think they were taking tea with the vicar not drinking in a tavern frequented by a cold-hearted devil with fangs."

Elliot ordered a bottle of Franconian wine which he had sampled once before and then turned his attention to Grace and Evelyn, who were busy chatting and laughing as though they had not a single care in the world.

"I think they're just relieved to be out of the carriage," Elliot said, doubting their babbling had anything to do with suppressing nerves.

The muscles in his shoulders were still painful to touch. But three weeks confined to such a small compact space—other than a few hours spent each night at various inns en route—had not affected his wife's cheerful countenance.

Alexander snorted. "As we all are. I don't think I'll be able to straighten my legs properly for a month. Every time I try, the joints in my knees crack."

Elliot chuckled but stepped closer and whispered, "We

will need to find a way of getting more blood while we're here. We must make it a priority once we've found Leo. An extra dose or two will soon lubricate your stiff bones."

Alexander glanced around the room, not bothering to hide his disdainful sneer. "I don't know why, but I feel like throttling every person in here for not alerting strangers to the monster walking amongst them. Perhaps an extra dose would also help me to maintain my calm composure."

Elliot laughed. "Calm composure? Despite your best efforts, you always appear angry and highly irritated. Unless you're talking to Evelyn, and then you look like an altar boy who has just witnessed an epiphany."

Alexander gave a sinful smirk. "Well, she is utterly divine. She's a saint sent to soothe all my gripes and woes. I'd be lost without her."

A frisson of fear shot through Elliot's body when he glanced at Grace's angelic face. She met his gaze and smiled, but he imagined sharp fangs overhanging her bottom lip, the whites of her eyes littered with ugly red veins. "What the hell were we thinking? We should have left our wives in London," he said as his chest grew tight and he found it hard to swallow.

"I hope you're not blaming me."

"Of course not," Elliot scoffed. "We were both weak and pathetic when it came to making demands. It seems both ladies do not respond well to orders."

Alexander gave a weak chuckle, but Elliot could sense his anxiety. "Grace only had to straighten your cravat and flutter her lashes, and you were pinning like a puppy."

"I seem to recall as soon as Evelyn touched your cheek you fell to your knees and surrendered," Elliot countered.

Alexander raised an arrogant brow. "So, I'm in love with

my wife. Indeed, I shall be glad of a little privacy this evening."

"I wouldn't imagine you'll get to spend much time in your room tonight." Elliot winced as he anticipated Alexander's growl of protest. "We need to search for Leo. There'll be plenty of time to rest come the morning."

"That bloody idiot," Alexander snarled. "He has a lot to answer for. Had it not been for his inflated ego, I would be nestled up in bed with nothing to do but think of new ways to entertain Evelyn."

"Have you tried to tune into his thoughts?" Elliot asked. He was still struggling to come to terms with the fact Leo had raced off to Bavaria, with the intention of punishing the woman who had ruined their lives.

Alexander shook his head. "I can't hear a thing."

"Me neither." Elliot gave a weary sigh. He could pick up the faint strains of desire but assumed it must be the voice of his own inner frustrations. "You don't think ... think she's killed him?"

"If she hasn't, I damn well will." Alexander straightened and threw his hands up. "Forgive my insensitive outburst. I'm just so damn annoyed with him I can hardly contain it. Three weeks cramped in a carriage has done little to temper my foul mood."

"I understand. I feel your anger," Elliot said with some sympathy, "just as I feel your fear. And like you, I'm struggling to hide my contempt for everyone here. I had hoped never to come back again."

Perhaps they should have stayed in England. Leo was man enough to make his own decisions and reap the consequences. But due to the nature of their affliction, the bond forged between them could not be broken. If roles were reversed, Elliot knew Leo would not rest until they were reunited.

The proprietor's cough disturbed his reverie. Elliot paid the man and took the goblets and the black bell-shaped bottle over to the table.

"Well?" Evelyn said as soon as they'd sat down. "Is he here? Has anyone seen him? Please tell me we haven't travelled all this way for nothing."

Elliot suppressed his anxiety and tried to infuse a level of confidence into his tone. "Apparently, he does have a room here and has paid until the end of the week, though the proprietor cannot recall the last time he saw him. His carriage is in the courtyard behind the tavern and his coachman, Chambers, has not seen him, either."

Grace turned to Evelyn. "Perhaps one of us should talk to the maid, offer an incentive if she agrees to take us up to his room."

"That's an excellent idea," Elliot said as his chest burst with pride at his wife's logical suggestion. "Although I doubt there is only one."

Evelyn smirked. "What? You doubt there is only one maid or that he has only taken one to his bedchamber?"

"Both," Elliot replied with some amusement as he poured the ladies a drink. "Perhaps Leo thought to use his licentious ways to taunt the devil from her lair."

Grace raised a curious brow. "You still believe that is the only reason she poisoned you all with her tainted blood?"

"We share no other commonality."

"Except for the fact we're all peers," Alexander added.

Evelyn smiled. "And you're all English. Perhaps she has a thorough dislike for arrogant foreigners."

"Then that would include most of the gentlemen in London," Alexander said, the corners of his mouth twitching.

Elliot was pleased they could make light of such a terri-fying situation. Doing so helped suppress his anxiety, gave him hope they would find Leo safe and well and could all go home and continue as before. However, there was a strange feeling in the air: an icy breeze capable of penetrating through the hardiest resolve. He suspected their lives would be altered by any further interaction with the woman who had stolen their humanity.

Evelyn tapped Grace on the arm, whispered in her ear, and they both scanned the boisterous crowd, suddenly gasping as they stared at a woman clearing tables.

"You did say Leo is attracted to a particular type of woman." Evelyn nodded to the petite golden-haired wench. "Perhaps we should ask her. I would wager a year's clothing allowance he has taken her up to his chamber."

"We will say he is our brother," Grace added. "That way she will be more forthcoming. We'll say he has an illness where he forgets things, and we grew worried when he did not return home."

Evelyn nodded. "Come on."

Alexander leant across the table and put his hand on his wife's arm. "I do not think it is wise to go off alone."

"I'm not alone. Grace is with me, and we will not leave the tavern. Besides, if you go out tonight to search for Leo we will be alone then."

Elliot put a hand of reassurance on his friend's shoulder. "I'm sure they will be fine." He glanced at Grace. "If you fail to return within ten minutes, I am coming to find you."

They watched the ladies converse with the serving wench, their friendly countenance helping to secure her co-operation. Grace glanced back over her shoulder and gave a confident grin.

"Damn, I still can't believe how lucky I am," Elliot said.

The thought of losing such a precious treasure caused a dull ache in his chest. "Do you remember what you asked me in the garden of Evelyn's aunt's house?"

Alexander narrowed his gaze. "What, that I want you to kill me should anything happen to Evelyn? I have not changed my mind. Our pact still stands."

"Then I want you to do the same for me." Elliot had never been happier than he had during the two months he had spent with Grace. "I love her deeply and cannot envisage a life without her."

Alexander sat back in the chair. "I understand completely. Does Grace know you're immortal?"

"Of course not." He knew such a revelation would upset her, particularly when she discovered he would never age. "I'll tell her at some point, just not yet. After all we've been through, I'd like a few years of peace and happiness."

"The words have almost slipped from my lips many times," Alexander confessed. "But I cannot bear to see Evelyn's eyes filled with sorrow. While I do not wish to deceive her, I am too weak to admit the truth."

Elliot forced a smile. "I'm glad our wives have become such good friends. It is important to have support from someone who understands your plight."

Alexander nodded. "You know I would like nothing more than to lock Evelyn away at Stony Cross and keep her all to myself. But I am beginning to think it is not healthy for her. When we return to England, I am considering spending a few months of the year in London. I would like her to see more of Grace. If you're in agreement, we will time our trips to coincide with yours."

Elliot could not hide his surprise. "Then some good has come from spending three weeks together in a carriage," he chuckled. "We are family in every sense of the word. I think it is important to support one another. With such a debilitating affliction such as ours, we should remain close."

Alexander gave a weary sigh. "All we need to do now is find that wayward brother of ours and drag him home. Perhaps on our return, we should trawl the ballrooms in the hope of finding a lady willing to tame him."

"She would have to have golden hair and a desire to let him drink her blood," he said in jest. "I doubt it will be too difficult to find someone suitable."

"No. It will be bloody impossible."

They both laughed, but Elliot's mood darkened when Grace and Evelyn appeared. Their grim faces sent a bolt of fear shooting through him.

"Is something amiss?" he said as soon as they approached the table.

They both sat down. Grace nodded to Evelyn, who said, "Leo left the tavern two nights ago. The wench said she spent time with him in his chamber, saw him climb into a carriage and has not seen him since. All of his clothes and belongings are still upstairs."

A hard lump formed in Elliot's throat and he couldn't speak.

"Does she know whose carriage it was?" Alexander asked.

"It belongs to Frau Lockwood."

"Thank the Lord." Elliot was able to breathe freely again. "More than likely he's found a mistress and forgotten all about this absurd need for revenge."

Grace winced at his reaction and said after a slight hesitation, "Frau Lockwood lives in the castle high up on the hill. She has lived there for ten years. Frau Lockwood has golden hair, wears a dark cloak and is seen mostly at night."

81

With trembling hands, Elliot grabbed the bottle, filled his goblet and downed the potent liquid so fast he almost retched.

Grace sighed. "The wench believes she may have been dreaming, but she thought Leo had a sword strapped to his back. We found an empty scabbard under his bed."

"But why would she allow him into her carriage knowing he had a sword?" Alexander shook his head. "It doesn't make any sense."

"You know what this means?" Elliot sucked in a breath. "I will have to go up to the castle. I can't leave here until I know what's happened to him."

"I'll come with you," Alexander said.

"Perhaps we should all go together," Evelyn suggested.

"No!" both gentlemen cried in unison, aware they had attracted the attention of a few curious locals.

"No," Elliot whispered firmly. "You will both stay here. You promised you would else I would not have let you come. Do not make me compel you to do so."

Grace's eyes grew wide. "You wouldn't."

When it came to their safety, there was no room for negotiation.

"We both will," Alexander added ignoring Evelyn's irate stare.

"We will all go to my room," Elliot commanded. "We will go to my room now without hesitation."

They escorted the ladies to Elliot's room, used mind manipulation on their wives to keep them there as they could not risk them coming up to the castle. Then they compelled them to lock the door behind them.

"I'm going to have to make Evelyn forget about this else she will find a way to punish me. I know it."

Elliot patted his friend on the back. "I hated doing it, too, but their safety has to be our priority. They will understand.

Besides, come the morning they will be free to do as they please."

"You assume we'll return tonight?"

"I sincerely hope so. But that is why I told you only to force her to stay in the room until sunrise. If we fail to return, I have instructed Gibbs to take them home." Elliot removed his pocket watch and glanced at the time before replacing it. "We'll have nine hours to get there and back. It should be plenty of time. But it would be wise to note how long it takes us to reach the castle, should anything unexpected occur."

They headed out into the night, followed the path leading up through the forest. No clouds littered the inky sky and the light from the full moon cast a silvery-blue hue to illuminate their way.

"What will we do if she's killed him?" Alexander asked, vocalising the words Elliot dared not think let alone speak.

"Then we will have two choices. We kill her, or we return to the tavern, jump into the carriage and head back to England."

They fell silent. The crunching of twigs underfoot and the rustling of leaves in the breeze did nothing to distract from the gravity of their situation.

"If it comes to it," Elliot continued after contemplating how best to proceed, "if we've got no choice but to fight, then I want you to let me deal with it. I want you to leave, take Grace and Evelyn and get as far away from this place as you can."

"I won't leave you," Alexander declared. "I could not live with it on my conscience."

"You must think of Evelyn. And you must promise me you will take care of Grace." Hell, just saying the words caused his airways to constrict.

"Hopefully, we will find Leo locked in the dungeon

sucking on the blood of rats. The devil woman will have left the key in the door, and we'll all be in our beds come the morning."

Elliot admired his friend's optimism even though he knew it was feigned purely for his benefit. "I'm sure you're right."

They trudged on for another fifteen minutes before reaching the stone bridge leading up to the castle. Staying close to the wall, they crept through the arched gatehouse and headed into the open courtyard.

Elliot jabbed his finger at the huge oak door, the entrance as tall as two men. "Is that the only way in?"

Alexander shrugged. "I can't remember much about my time here and often question if my terrified mind concocted some of the images." He glanced up and scanned the old building. "They built the castle on the cliff as a means of protection. I doubt there would be any other entrance."

Elliot glanced up at the eerie facade rising up from the rocky crag, at the winged gargoyles protruding from the stone walls, at the slate conical spires glistening in the moonlight. In its entirety, the medieval building roused feelings of grief, despair, and utter hopelessness.

Swallowing down his apprehension, Elliot said, "Well, I have no intention of scaling the wall, so we've no choice but to knock the door."

"Heaven knows how many of them are living in there." Alexander scoured the row of windows above, his tone conveying a hint of fear.

"Well, we will achieve nothing standing on the doorstep. And we are one of them now. We must remember we have strength and power of our own. Besides, we have too much at stake to walk away, too much to lose."

Alexander nodded. "I agree. Knock the door, and we will compel her servant to let us in."

They stood in front of the arched entrance. Elliot pursed his lips as he raised the heavy knocker and let it fall. The hollow thud echoed through the hallway beyond. They stepped back and waited, but no one came. He tried again before turning the iron ring that served as a handle, surprised to find it opened without protest.

"Perhaps they rarely have visitors," he said, noting the confusion marring Alexander's brow.

"Or perhaps they have nothing to fear as there's an army of nightwalkers beyond this door all desperate for blood." Alexander's thoughts were bordering on irrational.

Elliot pushed the door wide enough for them to slip inside, the creaks and groans a reflection of its size and age. Peering into the dark hall, Elliot was relieved to find it empty.

"You've been in here before," he whispered to Alexander. "Where would she take him?"

"I remember climbing a spiral staircase up to a tower room that overlooked the village. Other than that, I recall nothing else."

Elliot pointed to the corridor leading off to the right. "If I've got my bearings, that would mean we need to proceed this way."

They walked stealthily through the hall, over the ornately engraved paving: dusty memorial stones for the dead. Climbing the first staircase they came to, they wandered through wide corridors littered with paintings of solemn-looking ancestors, colourful tapestries of biblical scenes. A vast array of free-standing candelabras lined their way, though the candles were unlit.

Upon hearing the sound of booted footsteps, they hid inside a curtained recess, peered at the hulking fellow trudging along oblivious to the intruders.

When they reached the narrow spiral staircase, Alexander

tapped him on the shoulder. "I remember those torch shaped wall sconces and the stained glass window at the top. It's this way."

They had taken but a few steps when they heard the deep masculine groan. Elliot's heart skipped a beat. He stopped to listen, the accompanying words becoming clearer the more he focused.

"Oh, God, what are you doing to me?" The masculine voice begged for help, for mercy.

"I am giving you what you deserve. I am giving you everything you deserve," came the devil woman's wicked reply.

Without any doubt, Elliot knew the man she held captive was Leo. Relief coursed through him. Leo was alive but the golden-haired creature that had claimed their humanity took pleasure in torturing him.

"We need to save him," Elliot whispered. "He will be too weak to help us, but we must overpower her."

Alexander nodded, and they moved quietly up the stone steps, stopped at the top and peered through the open doorway.

The sight that met them was more horrifying than Elliot had imagined. Leo's arms were tied to the bedposts, evoking memories of the way she had tied him to the iron rings embedded into the walls of the mausoleum. Amidst the mounds of crumpled sheets, the evil temptress had straddled Leo's naked body as she sucked and nibbled on his neck like a starving woman would a juicy slab of beef.

Leo's head fell back against the pillow. He closed his eyes as a weak moan fell from his trembling lips. "Oh, God help me." Obviously, his poor friend could not take any more.

The devil woman raised her head, and Elliot could see the blood trickling from two circular wounds on Leo's neck.

Anger flared. To witness such a cruel form of punishment made him want to retch. But he had to be strong for Leo. Noticing the sword on the floor by the bed, he knew he could reach it before she would have time to react.

He waited until she resumed her wicked ministrations, until she bent her head and licked the blood from his neck with the tip of her tongue as she writhed on top of his helpless body.

Elliot nodded to Alexander and then crept into the room, grabbed the sword from the floor and with two hands thrust it high above his head. "Get your filthy bloodthirsty fangs off him."

Leo's eyes flew open, growing wide with shock. "Elliot?" His gaze drifted to the doorway. "Alexander?"

The devil woman gave an ear-piercing scream, grabbed the sheet and held it to her bare breasts as she scrambled to Leo's side. Elliot noticed Leo's fangs protruding, the sharp tips coated crimson.

"What the hell are you doing here?" Leo asked without the slightest hint of gratitude for the hundreds of miles they had travelled, for the weeks spent cramped inside a bloody carriage with barely enough air to breathe.

"What do you think we're doing here? We've come to rescue you from the evil clutches of the golden-haired devil."

CHAPTER 10

"*D*amn it. Quick, untie me, Ivana." Leo noted Elliot's look of utter confusion. "It is not what it seems," he said as guilt flared.

"Ivana?" Elliot's contempt for the woman who had turned him was evident in his expression and his tone. "You're calling her by her given name?"

"Put the sword down," Leo said as Ivana freed his right hand. He touched the pads of his fingers to his neck. The damp, sticky residue clung to the tips. Bloody hell. It must look even worse than he suspected.

Alexander stepped forward. "What is this?" he asked through gritted teeth as he waved his hand at the rumpled sheets. His wide eyes surveyed Leo's naked form, falling to the hard evidence of his arousal. "Please tell me it is not what it looks like."

Hell, Leo didn't even know where to start. It had taken hours to hear Ivana's lengthy explanation, and now he had to try to make his brothers understand the reason for his betrayal in a matter of minutes.

It didn't help that Elliot stood frozen to the spot, the look of disgust on his face like a blunt blade twisting in Leo's gut.

Leo glanced back and forth between the men he called his brothers. "Just give me a chance to explain."

"We have travelled for three weeks to find you," Elliot sneered as Ivana freed his other hand before rearranging the sheets to protect his modesty. "I thought you were being tortured. I stood outside the blasted door prepared to give my life to save you. And all the time—" He stopped abruptly and shook his head. "All the time you're cavorting with the devil woman who stripped us of our humanity."

Anger flared in Leo's chest. "Don't call her that."

Elliot ignored him. "Move out of the way, Leo, so I can put an end to this once and for all."

Despite Alexander's annoyance, he turned to Elliot. "Let us hear what he has to say before you do something you may later regret."

Elliot snorted. "Half an hour ago you wanted to kill him for all the trouble he has caused. Now you plead for clemency? If there is one thing I can't abide, it is a damn hypocrite." He nodded towards Leo. "Look at him. Look at his blood-stained fangs. Look at the mark burnt into his chest. This creature has ruined our lives. She has poisoned our brother's mind, and I'll not rest until she pays for what she's done."

Ivana cleared her throat. "From what Leo has told me, it seems your life has never been better. There are not many men who can claim to have found their one true mate." She sounded confident but he could feel her shaking beside him. "The gentleman I met in the mausoleum was blind to the beauty of love."

Elliot lunged forward, and they all gasped. "Do not dare speak to me of such things. What would you know of it?

Because of you, I must watch helplessly as the woman I love slowly fades away from me with each passing year. I will never forgive you for that." Taking a deep breath, he said, "Move aside, Leo."

"If you will only listen to what she has to say," Leo pleaded, "as I have done. I have witnessed things that have made me alter my views about what happened here."

Elliot raised the sword an inch higher. "Nothing anyone could say or do would make me change my opinion. Nothing could eradicate the four years of agony. What's worse is she has changed you again. The man I know would never betray the brotherhood. The man I know would not degrade himself by bedding the woman we all despise."

"I *am* a changed man," Leo acknowledged. "I am not the same man I was before I came back here. But you need to know why, Elliot."

"I'll give you one more chance to move."

Leo swallowed. He could feel the roaring flames of anger burning in Elliot's chest. But he sensed his friend's pain, too. Casting doubt over everything they had believed to be true was bound to cause emotions to flare. It was unsettling, unnerving, and Elliot was scared.

"I cannot move, Elliot," he said with a heavy heart. "You will have to kill us both." He turned to Ivana, ignored the fact two men loomed over the bed. "I believe in you," he said, stroking her cheek. A smile touched his lips when he noticed the trickle of dried blood on her neck. She had tasted divine. Their joining had been everything she'd promised it would be, and more. "I understand your motives. If I must die, I will die here with you."

She covered his hand and smiled. "It is how it was always meant to be. We should never have been apart. I should have been stronger. I should have fought for us."

"It doesn't matter now. We have found each other again."
He turned to Elliot. "I appreciate the effort it took for you
both to come and find me. I would never have wanted to tear
you away from the women you love. But if this is the end,
then so be it."

It was as though the whole room stood suspended in a
moment of frozen stasis: no one moved, no one spoke, no one
dared to breathe. The air felt stale and stagnant.

After what seemed like an hour, Elliot threw the sword to
the floor, the clattering sound echoing through the chamber.
"You have made your choice," he said before turning on his
heels and storming out through the doorway.

Alexander stared at them, his expression solemn, grave.
"Is this truly what you want?"

Leo didn't want to side against his brothers, but he hoped
they would understand given time. "It is."

"You choose to be with her?" he asked somewhat incredulously.

"I do."

"It will be hard for Elliot to accept your decision."
Alexander swallowed audibly and focused his attention on
Ivana. "Do not mistake my calm countenance for approval. I
want to kill you with my bare hands for what you've done to
me. But I recognise the truth in your words. The man I used
to be was not capable of love. Sometimes we must experience
our darkest nightmares for us to appreciate the beauty of our
dreams."

"You, too, have found love then," Ivana said with a look
of wonder. "It is a precious gift to be treasured. In time, you
might come to understand why I had no choice but to
hurt you."

"Elliot's experience in the mausoleum still haunts him,
though he suppresses the feelings. There was something cold

and cruel about the way you behaved with him as opposed to us, which is why he will never forgive you."

Leo sat up. The need to defend her was strong. "You don't know all she has done for him, for—"

Ivana put her finger to his lips. "Hush. Now is not the time for confessions or revelations."

She could have let him blurt the truth as a way of defending her actions. She could have made Elliot feel foolish, cold-hearted. Calvino had taught him that one sees the true nature of a person when they are under attack. There were cowards. There were men quick to boast as a way of disguising their fear. And then there were those whose integrity commanded respect. Ivana cared for the children more than she cared for herself and Leo's heart swelled all the more for her.

"I had my reasons," she said, addressing Alexander. "But I was not myself that night. The tainted blood I'd drunk had affected my mind. Bitterness and resentment caused me to attack Elliot in such a brutal manner. But I cannot go back and change what happened."

Alexander looked to the floor. "I should go and find him. He has always been the strongest, most reliable one of us. He has never failed in his duty to the brotherhood, and I owe him a debt of gratitude for all he has done for me. You must give him time, Leo."

Alexander inclined his head and left the room.

Leo exhaled deeply.

Ivana threw her arms around him. She was shaking with suppressed emotion. "I thought he was going to kill me. My life flashed before my eyes and all I saw was pain and misery."

Leo took hold of her chin and tilted her face so he could look into her eyes. "What just happened between us was heavenly, Ivana. What you do for the children is the work of an angel. I am not saying what you did to us was right. But it's done with. And I can see you are working to readdress the balance."

"I fear the worst is yet to come."

He attributed her cryptic words to the guilt she felt, to the shock of being threatened with death for the second time in so many days. He supposed she never thought to see them all again, especially not together.

"I should go and speak to Elliot. Try to make him understand. He has been a huge part of my life for the last three years, and I would not be here without his support."

"I too must go," she said. "It's too late to read to the children, but I will call and see Herr Bruhn. I hate to think of him sitting alone all night, and I would like to check on Frau Bruhn."

Ivana kissed him once softly on the mouth.

"Will you go with Sylvester?" he asked, fearing what Elliot would do in his irrational state if he caught sight of her going out alone.

"Of course," she said, offering him a smile though it did not light up her face as it usually did. "You do not think I would walk through the forest while there are men intent on murder."

"Alexander will not hurt you." In truth, Leo was shocked at the earl's reaction. Alexander had no patience; his short temper made him volatile and often unpredictable. "He is angry, but then I have never seen him any other way unless he is with Evelyn."

"Evelyn? Is she the love he refers to?"

"Evelyn is his wife. I have known her for a short time, but I think of her as a sister."

Ivana sighed. "It eases my conscience to know that they

are loyal, loving gentlemen. That they love with their hearts, not their anatomy. To marry takes a great sacrifice and commitment, and it pleases me to know some good has come of it all."

Perhaps one day soon he would be ready to marry. Would he marry Ivana? He could not envisage sharing his heart or his bed with any other woman. Indeed, he could imagine them living together in the castle. He would buy another house, somewhere in France, somewhere where all the brothers and their wives could spend the winter months.

Leo shook his head. Even in his wild imagination, he had never expected to dream of such things. Indeed, he rarely ever suffered from bouts of sentimentality.

"Marriage does not seem so daunting to me anymore," he said in a bid to gauge her reaction. "Since witnessing the pleasure gleaned from such a union, I find it has some appeal."

Ivana stared at him, swallowed deeply but offered no form of encouragement, no hint that she would welcome a declaration. "Marriage is not for everyone. Some things are better left as they are."

Her response sounded cold, detached. But then she was a woman ruled by her heart, and he had not mentioned love. Was it love he felt or merely an overwhelming need to sate the lust ravaging his mind and body? Did it have something to do with a desperate need to remember what they'd meant to each other before? Only time would tell. In the past, he had often found it difficult to distinguish between the swelling in his chest and that of his cock.

"I must go. Herr Bruhn will be worried." Ivana climbed out of bed and scoured the floor, rummaged through the pile of discarded garments.

The branding mark on her hip drew his attention. Why hadn't he noticed it before?

"The mark on your hip," he said as she threw her chemise over her head and wiggled into it. "Is it the same as mine?"

Her face grew solemn, her complexion pale, ashen. "Yes. It is the same."

He stared at the thorny cross in a circle of twine. "How did you come by it?" It suddenly occurred to him that someone must have bitten Ivana, too. She must have been human once; an innocent young woman lured by a devil.

"The same way you did." She was being deliberately vague. "It is a symbol of the suffering we must endure."

"Who turned you?" he asked bluntly.

She glanced at the floor. "It is a long story. Too long to begin when we have so many other things we must do this night."

Curiosity burned away. "I have often wondered about its purpose." When she returned from her visit to Herr Bruhn, they would sit by the fire, and she would tell him everything.

Disdain flashed in her eyes. "It is to remind me I am cursed, to remind me my fangs are an instrument of death. Like the crown of thorns, they tear into flesh, inflict nothing but pain and misery. It is a sign of degradation and mockery. It heralds the fall of man."

"And so you branded me for the same reason? To remind me of all that I am."

She did not answer at first. "I branded Elliot and Alexander for the same reason."

Why could she not speak plainly? Why was every question met with a cryptic response?

"And what of me, Ivana? Why did you brand me?"

"There is no time now. We will talk when I return."

He sensed there were still many secrets buried beneath

her charming countenance, perhaps harrowing experiences she struggled to reveal.

Ivana stepped into her dress, pulled it up and fastened the buttons, brushed the knots from her hair, washed her hands and face in the bowl of cold water. She never spoke a word, never glanced in his direction.

Well, he would give her something to contemplate during the carriage ride through the forest.

"I prefer to think of the mark differently," he said, as he had never been overly concerned with it and certainly did not see it in the same grotesque way she did. "To me, it is a symbol of hope. A sign that goodness can prevail even in the darkest times."

Ivana gave a weak smile. She walked over to him, took his hand and kissed it gently, closed her eyes briefly as though searing the moment to her memory.

"Faith is a powerful thing, Leo. Let us hope you have enough for both of us. I have a feeling we will soon be in need of divine intervention. We are going to need all the help we can get."

CHAPTER 11

"*D*o you think we should have told them everything we know?" Grace said as she stood at the bedchamber window staring up at the ominous building towering above the trees. The sight of the conical spires caused a deep sense of foreboding.

Evelyn came to stand at her shoulder. "The wench told us nothing other than Frau Lockwood visits a house in the village every evening. If anything, it was better we remained silent."

Grace turned to face her. "How so?"

"Think about it. If Frau Lockwood leaves the castle to visit the elderly gentleman, then it will be easier for them to rescue Leo. With any luck, their paths will not even cross."

"I do hope you're right." Grace could not hide the nervous edge to her tone. While Elliot had told her about the terrifying night in the mausoleum, she believed painful feelings of bitterness and resentment still lay buried deep within.

How would he fare when forced to confront the woman he blamed for stealing his humanity? What if the experience changed him? Grace wanted everything to be as perfect as those first few weeks in Yorkshire.

"I have a strange feeling everything will work out just fine," Evelyn said confidently. "In truth, I think they needed to come back here. They needed to confront the demons of the past."

"That's what scares me." Grace glanced out of the window; the haunting sight of the full moon caused a shiver to run down her spine. "What if they don't come back? What if they find others with the same affliction living in the castle? What if they want to drink blood openly and freely without the need to hide it from the world?"

Evelyn grasped her upper arms. "Your thoughts are irrational." She forced Grace to look at her. "Elliot loves you. You will need to control your emotions if we are going to be any help to them."

Help to them?

What on earth could they do when faced with a devil in the guise of a temptress?

"What? Do you have a plan in mind?" Grace noted the sly smirk playing on Evelyn's lips. "You do! I have seen that mischievous look in your eye numerous times before."

Evelyn's smirk turned into a beaming grin. "Of course. Why do you think I told you to shape the candle wax and put a blob in each ear?"

The mere mention of wax caused the itching to return. Grace scratched at her ear convinced remnants were still lodged inside the small canal. "I assumed you knew they would be over-protective. I assumed you would take umbrage at being manipulated, at losing your free will."

"I refuse to be treated like a child," Evelyn said with a firm nod. "If I want to risk my life to save the man I love, then that is my choice to make."

"I must say I am somewhat relieved. Every minute spent standing by this window feels more like a day. Another hour and I would be fit for Bedlam."

Evelyn took her hand and patted it gently. "Well, we would not want that. Now before we can do anything, we must check to see if the wax plug worked. When Elliot commanded you to stay in the room, did you do what I said?"

Grace nodded. "I hummed a tune in my head and stared at him blankly." It had not been an easy task, but it helped that she imagined she was listening to her sister, Caroline.

"Good. Hopefully, the wax will have helped to muffle the sound."

"It must have worked, as I struggled to follow the conversation around the table. What made you think of using candle wax?"

"I don't know. The thought just popped into my head. I recalled that in the Greek tale *Odyssey*, Circe tells Odysseus to make plugs for their ears from beeswax so they would not fall prey to the sirens song." Evelyn shrugged. "I hoped it would work in the same way, but I am a little sceptical."

Grace gave her a hug. It was the only way she knew to express her pride in her friend's ingenious plan. "I would never have thought of something so clever. If it had been left up to me, we'd still be sat in this room come the morning."

Evelyn rubbed Grace's upper arms as she stepped back. "Let us see if it worked before you offer any more praise for my inventiveness."

They turned and looked at the door, took hesitant steps towards it as though they expected to find a jeering crowd surrounding the hangman's scaffold on the other side.

Evelyn turned the key, grabbed the handle and exhaled. "Well, here goes." She opened the door and waved her hand for Grace to step over the threshold.

"Elliot will be furious with me if this works," Grace said, imagining the look on his face if he returned to find their room empty. Taking a deep breath, she stepped out into the hall. The sudden rush of satisfaction made her jump and clap her hands. "It worked. Good heavens."

Evelyn chuckled nervously. "What are the chances it worked for you but not for me? Alexander can be very domineering though he often struggles to form coherent sentences when I look at him in a certain way. Let's hope his mind was on other things and his words lacked the conviction needed."

With ease and with a cheer of elation, Evelyn joined Grace out in the hall.

"It's rather gratifying to know we are capable of weaving magic of our own," Evelyn said, looking terribly pleased with herself.

Grace straightened and, with a renewed sense of confidence, said, "So, we have managed to evade our captors. What now?"

Evelyn thought for a moment. "We will visit the elderly gentleman who lives at the end of the street. The wench said he cares for the orphan children of the village. So we will say we have come at Frau Lockwood's behest and wish to make a financial contribution to the cause."

"What if Frau Lockwood comes to see him while we are there?"

"The wench said she goes to see the children. Surely they'll be tucked up in their beds at this late hour. Besides, I doubt she would cause us any harm while in the presence of witnesses. She also said that the children are often seen playing outside, so they do not possess the same affliction."

Grace found the whole thing baffling. It was as though Frau Lockwood and the devil woman were two different people. On one hand she appeared to be caring and nurturing.

On the other hand, she was capable of the most evil, inhumane acts.

"Why do you think she goes to visit them?" Grace asked curiously.

Evelyn threw her hands up. "I haven't the faintest idea. But I remember the feeling I had in my stomach the night I found Alexander at Stony Cross. My mind told me to take a different path, but my feet refused to follow. I have a similar feeling now. We have no choice but to go where our hearts lead us."

"Well, if nothing else, I should like to hear about the children. The gentleman must surely be kind and generous for giving them a home."

What was the worst that could happen? The devil woman could poison their blood, could infect them with the same debilitating affliction. Grace could cope with anything as long as she had Elliot by her side. Nothing could be as terrifying as the thought of losing him.

"Herr Bruhn," Evelyn suddenly chirped. "That's what she said his name was."

"Come, let us get our capes," Grace said with some enthusiasm. They would go now while she felt confident. "It has started raining again, and there's every chance the old man won't even let us in."

Ten minutes later, they stood outside the door of Herr Bruhn's house, threaded their arms and huddled together as a way to suppress the shivering. Evelyn knocked once, knocked again when he failed to answer.

"Perhaps he is busy with the children," Grace said, glancing at the upstairs window.

"As I said, they are bound to be in bed at this late hour."

Evelyn was about to knock for a third time when they heard the shuffling of feet behind the door, followed by the clunk of a lock opening. As the door creaked ajar a few inches, they saw the old man peering out at them, confusion marring his already wrinkled brow.

"Good evening, Herr Bruhn," Evelyn said with all the confidence of a lady of her station, although they had already agreed not to use their titles. "I am sorry to call when it is so late. I am Evelyn Cole, and this is my good friend Grace Markham. Frau Lockwood told us about the children and asked us to call and speak to you about making a financial contribution to your worthy cause."

Herr Bruhn's apprehensive gaze scanned them from head to toe. "Frau Lockwood asked you to call?"

"Yes, we met her up at the castle on the hill."

Herr Bruhn's countenance suddenly brightened. "Of course, of course." He opened the door wide. "Please, come in out of this nasty rain."

The old man hung up their damp capes and escorted them into a small parlour.

"Oh, what miserable weather," Evelyn said, patting her hair.

"Please, take a seat by the fire." He gestured to the two chairs hugging the hearth. "I shall just go and get a stool so I can join you."

They sat down, grateful for the heat generated by the roaring flames.

Grace leant forward and whispered, "It's rather small considering he has so many children to care for."

"Yes," Evelyn replied with a weary sigh. "But it feels comfortable and homely. I could happily spend my days snuggled in this chair reading a book."

Herr Bruhn shuffled back into the room, placed the wooden stool between the two chairs and sat down. "I must say it is a joy to have company this evening." He suddenly shot to his feet. "Forgive my rudeness. I have not offered you refreshment."

Grace waved her hand. "Please sit down. We have only just eaten."

Herr Bruhn nodded as he settled back into his seat. The dark circles framing his eyes marred his cheerful countenance. His lips were dry and chapped, his complexion pale and drawn. A man of his years must surely struggle to cope with energetic infants.

"Frau Lockwood spoke very highly of the work you do here," Evelyn said.

"I do not see it as work. The children are my family. Frau Lockwood is an angel sent to do the Lord's bidding. Without her tireless efforts, we would not be able to care for them as we do."

Grace swallowed down her surprise. How could a woman be an angel to one man and a devil to another? Perhaps there had been some mistake.

"Does Frau Lockwood come to visit you every evening?" Grace asked, wondering what the old man knew of her affliction.

"Yes, yes. She comes to read to the children and to put them to bed. It gives me a chance to eat my supper and tend to my wife who is still ill in bed."

Grace felt a rush of relief, quickly replaced by a feeling of dread. As the children appeared to be in their beds, Frau Lockwood must have already been and left. She would be on her way back to the castle.

"She told us she cannot help you during the day, which is why we thought we could contribute. With the extra funds, you could employ someone else to assist you." Grace was sincere in her offer. The old man looked so tired and weary she felt compelled to help. Judging by the look of pity on Evelyn's face, she was of a similar mind.

Herr Bruhn clapped his frail hands. "That would be wonderful. Frau Lockwood is so busy during the day, and she does so love to read her folk tales. I know she worries terribly, worries that she cannot do more for them."

"We were told the children are orphans," Evelyn said, "but what happened to their parents? Was there an illness in the village?"

Grace knew why Evelyn had sought to pry. Were their parents suffering from the same terrible affliction? Was guilt the reason for Frau Lockwood's involvement?

Herr Bruhn narrowed his gaze. "Frau Lockwood did not tell you?"

"No. Perhaps she thought it would be best if you did."

"Ah, I see." The old man sighed. "She finds it too distressing to speak of. Perhaps it is not for the ears of such gently bred ladies."

Evelyn sat forward. "We would like to understand."

Herr Bruhn was silent for a moment and then nodded. "There is a waterfall but a mile or two from here, high up in the hills. They claim the waters flow from Heaven. That they have a spiritual potency to heal all wounds. Some fifty years or more an Englishman stumbled upon this place on his journey to Italy. He spoke of the magical waters, of the beauty to behold here and ever since it has been one of the attractions for the fancy lords on their *Grand Tour*. Of course, it is all nonsense. It is just a mountain stream after all."

"Forgive me," Grace said, not meaning to be impertinent, "but what has that got to do with the children?"

"Many of the gentlemen who come here are on expeditions, expeditions of a debauched nature. They are not interested in the paintings, the beautiful statues or magnificent scenery. They care not for the mystical waters. Their interests lie in wine and women. They care not for the devastation they leave behind."

They were all silent for a moment. There was a gravity to his words, a hint of contempt. As always, Evelyn's logical mind deciphered his meaning.

"You mean these children are the offspring of English lords who pass through here?" she asked, and Grace could sense her apprehension while they waited for his answer.

"They are. The gentlemen move on. The women, well, some do too."

Grace put her hand to her throat. Poor little innocent hearts and minds discarded by men who were indifferent to their plight. Anger flared. If they were in London, she would call out the scoundrels for their callous disregard.

"I see," Evelyn said with a sigh.

"My heart feels heavy when I think of it," Herr Bruhn said, "but the children lift my spirits."

Grace smiled. "They must truly be a blessing to you."

"They are," he nodded. "Would you care to see them? They are sleeping, but it would not hurt to peer around the door."

Grace locked gazes with Evelyn. She knew they were both struggling with various conflicting emotions and wondered if the same questions burned in Evelyn's chest. Had the golden-haired devil chosen to curse the men who behaved so recklessly? Had their husbands been just as cruel and indifferent during their adventures abroad? She could not imagine either Elliot or Alexander turning their back on a child. Indeed, she prayed there was a flaw in her logic. Perhaps she was not thinking clearly, her mind being some-what overwrought and irrational.

"Yes," Evelyn began, sucking in a deep breath. "We would like to see the children."

Herr Bruhn led them upstairs to a chamber at the far end of the landing. "This is where the girls sleep," he said, using both hands to ease the door from the jamb.

They peered inside at the two young girls sleeping in their wooden beds. Grace's heart lurched. They looked so serene, so utterly peaceful in slumber with their silky hair fanned across the pillows, with the comforting rise and fall of their chests as they drifted in and out of dreams. In those precious hours of sleep, all the people in the world were equal. There were no rules to separate them, no debilitating diseases to mark them as different. There were no emotions at play, no feelings of sadness or loneliness.

They crept back out into the hall.

"The boys sleep here," Herr Bruhn whispered, moving to the door nearest the stairs. "When they are not arguing that is."

A light rap on the front door captured their attention.

"I'll be but a minute," Herr Bruhn continued, leaving them alone while he went downstairs.

They tiptoed into the room. The boys looked just as angelic as the girls. Grace counted three beds.

Evelyn grabbed her arm. "We must do what we promised," she said quietly. "We must give Herr Bruhn money to support these children."

Grace swallowed down the lump that had formed in her throat. "I agree. You will think I am silly, but I have a feeling we were supposed to come here. Perhaps there is another side to the whole story. Perhaps our husbands have been negligent."

Evelyn shook her head. "No. I thought the very same thing when Herr Bruhn regaled the tale of the dissolute peers." Her expression darkened. "You don't think … I can't even form the words without choking back the tears."

"I know what you're thinking," Grace began. Her heart was racing so fast she thought it might burst from her chest. "But I know neither Elliot nor Alexander would have the heart to abandon a child."

The little boy in the nearest bed stretched his tiny arms above his head and yawned. He turned over to face them, mumbled something in his sleep. Grace couldn't help but stare. His hair was as black as night, the same colour and texture as Elliot's. She stepped closer until her knees touched the wooden frame. She examined the shape of his mouth, noted his ears had small lobes.

Evelyn came to stand at her side as they loomed over the boy.

"How old do you think he is?" Grace asked, part of her wishing the answer was five, part of her desperately wanting it to be three or four.

"I'm not sure," Evelyn whispered. "It's difficult to tell while he is tucked under the blankets."

They heard the creak of a floorboard behind them. "How old is this boy?" Grace whispered, directing her question to the man behind her shoulder.

"Christoph? He is three."

They both swung around, alarmed to hear the feminine voice. The goddess standing before them smiled. Her golden hair hung loosely about her shoulders. Grace noted that her eyes were a piercing blue, noted the absence of fangs.

"He will be four in a few days," Frau Lockwood said. "Indeed, he looks remarkably like his father, wouldn't you agree?"

CHAPTER 12

$\mathcal{I}$vana's gaze drifted over their stunned faces.

Perhaps it was wrong of her to scare them so. But she was angry. They had lied to Herr Bruhn, persuaded him to let them into his home. A mere hour ago their husbands had looked upon her with disdain. One of them had been ready to end her life.

"You need not fear me," she said, noting the way the muscles in their cheeks twitched, how they were possessed with a need to swallow continually. "Leo has told me much about you."

When she spoke, they could not help but stare at her teeth.

"Frau Lockwood." The lady with wide blue eyes and full lips smiled. "I am Evelyn, Alexander's wife." She gestured to the flame-haired lady at her side. "And Grace is married to Elliot."

Ivana sensed a certain strength of character emanating from them, although Evelyn appeared to be the most confident. It took an immense amount of courage to marry a gentleman with such a terrifying affliction. To love such a man took an open mind and a pure heart.

"Then you must call me Ivana. I have just had the pleasure of meeting your husbands again," she said, her irate mood mellowing, although she maintained an air of detachment. "Let us just say they were not at all pleased to see me."

Grace's eyes widened. "Did ... did you hurt them?"

Their husbands must have told them gory tales of the night a devil tainted their blood, so she could not blame them for thinking the worst.

Ivana smiled. "They were alive and well when my carriage passed them on the road heading back to the village."

Despite offering reassurance, a look of panic marred their pretty faces.

Grace glanced at her friend. "They will know we have left the room."

"It doesn't matter," Evelyn replied. "We have other more important things to think of now." She turned to Ivana. "Are there any other children here, children younger than Christoph?"

Ivana knew why she had asked. "No. There are no younger children."

A look of disappointment flashed in Evelyn's eyes.

"Your husbands, they should not have brought you to Bavaria." Ivana's tone rang with an ominous warning. "It is not safe here."

Evelyn raised her chin. "But you said we have nothing to fear."

"From me," Ivana clarified. "You have nothing to fear from me. Despite what your husbands have told you, I believed I had a justifiable reason for what I did to them." She glanced at Christoph stirring in his bed. "We cannot talk here. Let us step outside. Herr Bruhn knows nothing of my affliction, and I do not want to alarm him."

Grace glanced back over her shoulder. "Before we leave,

just tell me one thing. The boy, Christoph, is he Elliot's child?"

Ivana knew she should lie. Every terrible deed she'd committed had been done out of love for the children. It was her responsibility to protect them. But things had changed. The Bruhns were growing frailer by the day. Ivana's life dangled precariously in the hands of another. Who would care for the children then?

She would have to trust her instincts. She would trust Leo's word that these women were kind, loving and generous.

"Yes, Grace. The boy is Elliot's son."

Grace's hands flew up to cover her mouth as her legs buckled beneath her. "I … I cannot believe it of him." She sucked in a breath, her face growing pale, drawn. "He would not leave a child. I know he would not. He is a good man."

Evelyn put her hand to the lady's elbow, offered words of comfort and helped her to her feet.

"Elliot does not know he has a son." Ivana was overcome with the need to soothe the woman's fears.

"He … he doesn't know." Grace choked on the words as she shook her head. "He doesn't know," she repeated as she put her hand to her heart, her shoulders sagging with relief.

Ivana narrowed her gaze. "You seem pleased to discover he is ignorant of the fact."

"Oh, I am."

"You are not distraught to find your husband has an illegitimate child?"

"Heavens, no," Grace said as her countenance brightened. "We all have a past. Some things are forgivable when one considers the circumstances."

How interesting. Perhaps Leo had the measure of these women.

"Let us leave the children to sleep in peace," Ivana said as she gestured to the hall.

They led the way and Ivana followed, closing the bedchamber door gently behind her. They met Herr Bruhn at the bottom of the stairs.

"I thought I would leave you alone," he said, offering numerous nods. "It is too cramped up there for all of us." He turned to Ivana. "We missed you this evening. I hope you are well."

She offered him a warm smile. "Forgive me. I received some unexpected guests and must return to tend to their needs. Rest assured. I will be here tomorrow to read to them."

Ivana could feel Evelyn's curious gaze.

"Please, do not worry." Herr Bruhn turned to the wives of the men she had stripped of their humanity. "She thinks of nothing but the children. God bless her."

"We will come tomorrow, too," Evelyn said, casting a dubious glance at Ivana. "We would like to meet the children. We would like to bring some provisions, and a donation to help you care for their needs."

Herr Bruhn clasped his hands to his chest. "The Lord has blessed me with three wonderful angels." He inclined his head. "Thank you."

Guilt flared in her chest. Ivana hated deceiving the old man. But to tell him the truth would only rouse fear in his pious heart.

"Until tomorrow," Ivana said as she waited for the women to tie the ribbons on their cloaks.

Herr Bruhn opened the door. "Until tomorrow."

They walked along the street in silence before Grace stopped abruptly. "I want to take Christoph back to England."

Ivana knew it was only a matter of time before she asked.

"Of course. But I will need your husband to agree before I can even think of broaching the subject with the Bruhns."

"He will agree," she replied confidently.

Ivana gave a weary sigh. "There is the matter of his affliction to discuss. The boy must not know of his father's condition. Such a task would make life difficult."

"We will find a way to manage."

The thought of Christoph moving hundreds of miles away caused Ivana's heart to ache. But she could not be selfish. "Come to the castle tomorrow evening and we will speak then." Noticing the faint flicker of apprehension, she added, "Bring your husbands along with you. I fear we all have much to discuss."

The ladies stared at each other and then nodded.

Ivana inclined her head. "Forgive me. I am tired and must return home."

Evelyn raised her chin. "You said you passed Alexander and Elliot on the way down to the village. What of Leo?"

The mere mention of his name sent a flurry of excitement coursing through her. "He is waiting at the castle for my return."

"Is he your prisoner?" Grace asked apprehensively.

"No. He is there of his own free will. But I shall leave it to your husbands to explain. At this time of year, I visit the children at nine and shall be ready to receive you after ten. Until tomorrow."

Ivana turned and walked solemnly towards her carriage.

What a difference a few days could make to one's life. She did not like the uncertainty that came with change. But after reuniting with Leo, she knew nothing would ever be the same again. If Elliot proved worthy, Ivana would explain the circumstances to Herr Bruhn and let them take the boy. She would let them take Leo, too. He could not stay in Bavaria. They could not be together as she wished. It crossed her mind to go with him. But she could not travel further than ten miles from the castle.

Nikolai had seen to that.

Nikolai had seen to everything.

Grace stared at the cloaked figure walking along the quiet street. The rain had eased a little, the misty mizzle coating everything in a glistening sheen. The wind whipped Ivana's golden tresses about her face, but she did not raise her hood. The woman had the inherent beauty of a temptress but certainly not the heart of a devil.

"I am still struggling to absorb all that I have seen and heard this evening." Grace sighed. "Elliot has a son. I cannot believe it. Though I knew the truth the moment I laid eyes on him."

"I know." Evelyn smiled sympathetically. "I cannot believe we have met the golden-haired devil from Bavaria and are still standing to tell the tale. She was not as terrifying as I imagined."

"No," Grace replied dreamily. "Despite her confidence and the obvious strength that emanates from her, I think she looks sad, so very sad and lonely."

They walked towards the tavern.

"Did you see the expression on her face when you asked about Leo?" Grace continued.

"I recall seeing a similar expression on your face," Evelyn said with a chuckle. "The day we left the apothecary, and you said you would just call around to see Elliot but were gone all afternoon."

The memory of the time spent in Elliot's bedchamber came flooding back to warm her cold bones.

"It was rather a special afternoon," Grace said, feeling the heat touch her cheeks. "I don't know how I am going to find the courage to tell him about the child."

"All things happen as they are intended to. I am a firm believer in that. You will know what to say when the time comes. I wonder if—" Evelyn stopped abruptly, her attention distracted as Alexander came charging out of the tavern door.

Grace gasped. "I don't think I have ever seen him look so cross."

"Leave this to me," Evelyn whispered. "He is always rather amorous when he is angry."

"How the hell did you manage to leave your room?" Alexander yelled as he stopped directly in front of them. "Where the hell have you been?"

Evelyn stepped forward and placed her palm on his chest which worked to soothe his ragged breathing. "We're fine. There is nothing to worry about." She held her arms open and twirled around. "See. But I am tired and would like to go to our room and lie down."

A look passed between them. His heated gaze devoured her, and she gave a coy smile in response. The passion they shared shone from them like the brightest beacon, and Grace was thankful she could not hear the salacious nature of their thoughts.

"I suspect Elliot is just as angry," she said, feeling a sudden urge to race to her room, to soothe him, to take him into her eager body in a bid to delay the pain her revelation would cause.

"Angry does not even begin to describe how he feels." Alexander's sombre expression did not worry her. She had seen a similar look many times before.

"I should go to him."

A loud crashing caused them all to jump back as a candlestick came hurtling out of a bedchamber window. It landed with a clunk on the cobbled walkway, along with shards of broken glass.

"Good heavens!" Evelyn gasped as she clutched Alexander's arm.

A few men came running out of the tavern, tiptoed around the debris as they stared at the strange object on the ground.

"Elliot has completely lost his mind," Alexander said. "It has taken me the best part of an hour to calm him down and then when he came back to find you'd gone ..." He shook his head as though the event was too distressing to recount.

Grace did not wait to hear any more. She raced into the tavern, pushed past those eager to step outside to witness the commotion, tripped on the stairs in her hurry to reach her husband.

The door to their chamber was wide open. Elliot was sitting on the edge of the bed, slumped forward, holding his head in his hands.

"Elliot."

"I asked you not to leave."

Grace closed the door and came to sit by his side. "I'm sorry if I went against your wishes." She placed her hand on his back. "I did not mean to hurt you or make you angry. That's the last thing I would ever want."

When he looked up at her, it wasn't anger she saw in his eyes. She saw pain and anguish. "It seems I cannot trust anyone anymore." Bitterness infused his words. "It seems Leo couldn't wait to betray me. After everything I have done for him."

"But Leo worships you," she said incredulously. "He

hangs on your every word. What has he done to warrant your contempt?"

Elliot's mouth curled up in disdain. "He has taken the golden-haired devil to his bed. Apparently, they formed an attachment when she turned him. Conveniently, he had forgotten all about it."

After noting the look of longing on Ivana's face at the mere mention of his name, Grace was not surprised. "What did Leo have to say?"

Elliot shrugged. "Nothing worthy of my attention. Oh, he followed me, tried to explain, but I'll be damned before I give him a chance to justify what he's done." He jumped up suddenly, thrust his hand through the mop of ebony hair as he paced the room. "God, it makes me retch just to think of them drinking each other's blood."

"They drank from each other?" While it might sound horrifying to some, Grace found the idea rather erotic. "Is Leo in love with her?" He must have developed a deep attachment if he had forgiven her for taking his humanity.

"Love?" Elliot mocked. "Neither of them would know the meaning of the word. Leo thinks with his cock." Upon hearing her gasp, he said, "Forgive me. I'm just so damn angry with him."

"I know what she did to you, and I do not blame you for despising her. But I do not think Ivana is the devil you make her out to be."

Elliot stopped abruptly, gazed at her beneath hooded lids. "Ivana? I did not tell you that was her name."

Grace swallowed. She would not lie to him. "We met Ivana at Herr Bruhn's house when she came to visit the children."

"You met her?" Elliot took a step closer, his wide eyes

scanning every inch of her body. "If she laid a hand on you then—"

"We spoke to her. That is all. Herr Bruhn said—"

"Who the blazes is Herr Bruhn? And how the hell did you manage to leave this room?"

Grace wasn't sure which question to address first. "I used wax in my ears, tried to ignore the sound of your voice."

"Wax? Why? You knew I would be frantic with worry if I came back to find you gone. Anything could have happened to you. She could have sunk her fangs into your neck. She could have—"

"But she didn't."

"If I cannot trust you to do what I ask—"

"You know you can trust me," she cried, rushing to him and taking his hand.

"Can I?" he sneered. "You left this room when I specifically asked you not to."

"You did not ask me, Elliot. You compelled me. It is not the same thing at all." Grace gave a frustrated groan. "If anything, I should be the one with a gripe. You forced me to do something against my will. Why would you do such a thing?"

He sucked in a breath, grasped her upper arms. "Because I love you," he blurted. "I cannot bear the thought of losing you. Without you, I have nothing. You are my world, Grace. Nothing else matters. Nothing."

The depth of emotion in his voice made her heart swell. He pulled her close, enveloped her in a warm embrace.

"I love you." She looked up and brushed her lips across his. She hated seeing him distraught. During their time in Yorkshire, he had been so happy, so carefree. She wished she could close her eyes and transport them back to that magical time and place.

But things were different now.

How was she to break the news to him that he had a son?

She pushed the thought aside for the moment. Elliot needed her to ease his fears, and she needed him too. Without another word, she pushed his coat from his shoulders, fumbled with the buttons on his waistcoat. Understanding her silent plea, they undressed each other with an urgency that expressed the raging passion they shared.

When he covered her naked body and pressed her down into the bed, she felt safe. When he filled her with each deep thrust, everything felt right again. A slower, more intimate expression of their love followed the frantic, lust-fuelled coupling. Both activities brought a soul-deep level of satisfaction. Both activities worked to relax them, to banish the anger and fear.

They lay together in sated silence, but Grace's thoughts were jumbled and chaotic. The curtain blew back and forth through the hole in the smashed window, and she shivered.

"I have something important to tell you," she said as she snuggled closer to Elliot's chest. "And I don't know how to begin."

Elliot rolled on to his side to face her, brushed the hair from her cheek. "Nothing could be as shocking as what I have witnessed tonight."

Grace sighed. "We went to visit Herr Bruhn. He takes care of the orphan children of the village, with Ivana's help and support." When his mouth twitched at the mere mention of her name, Grace said, "Just listen to me for a moment before you say anything."

Elliot smirked, a mischievous glint flashing in his eyes. "If my anger flares, will you soothe it away with your soft hands? Will you caress me and stroke me until I forget what roused my ire?"

"I will do all of those things and more if you will just listen to what I must tell you."

"Now you have my full attention."

She thought it best to come straight to the point. "As I said, Ivana supports the children. They are the offspring of English lords who frolic with tavern wenches, with desperate women from the village." Grace sucked in a breath, placed the palm of her hand over his heart. "That is why she bit you. To stop gentlemen like you fathering more children here."

"Bloody hell!" he cursed. "I suspected that was the reason." He fell silent for a moment while he contemplated her words. "I've never professed to be a saint, Grace. But I have always been careful in that regard."

"You were not careful enough, Elliot." She waited while he absorbed her words.

"Not careful?" he repeated, the faint lines across his brow growing more prominent. "What are you saying?"

She pressed her lips to his, pulled away and looked deeply into his brown eyes. "You have a son here," she whispered. "A beautiful boy aged three. He lives with Herr Bruhn. Ivana reads to him and tucks him up in bed every night."

He stared at her for the longest time, gulped and swallowed as he tried to speak. "Did ... did the golden-haired devil tell you this?"

"I knew the moment I saw him sleeping so sweetly in his bed. He is like you in so many ways. Ivana merely confirmed what I suspected."

He rolled on to his back, covered his eyes with his arm; his chest heaved as he struggled to control his breathing.

Grace knew he needed a little time to come to terms with what she had said. Throwing back the sheets, she climbed out of bed and pottered around the room. "I'll drape a blanket over the window. We cannot risk the morning sun streaming through."

"Come here. Come back to bed."

Grace turned to face him. Her heart lurched at his tortured expression, but she knew she must not surrender her body to him. "My touch will not banish the ghosts this time, my love. You must embrace your emotions. You must examine your heart and your conscience."

She could not ease his torment. She could not tell him how to react or what to do. If he made the wrong decision, if he chose to ignore his responsibilities then a part of her would not forgive him.

"I do not know what to think or feel." He sat up, leant back against the pillow and dragged his palm down his face. "Who … where is his mother?"

"You must ask Ivana. You need to hear the story from her lips. Then you must meet your son. Only then will you know what to do. Only then will the answer become clear to you."

He stared at her, his eyes conveying many unspoken words. "I … I don't want to lose you."

Graced rushed over to the bed. She tried to kiss away all of his doubts and fears. "You will never lose me, Elliot. We are bound together. Know that I will support you if you decide to take your son home."

Elliot shook his head as his gaze drifted over her face. "You are a shining light in a world full of misery."

Grace smiled. "And you are the most honest, kind and generous man I have ever known. Tomorrow we are to go to the castle. Ivana said we have many things to discuss. Listen to her, open your heart to your friend and brother and allow him the freedom to be happy."

"You do not ask for much," he mocked.

"Anyone can express anger, but it takes strength and

courage to show forgiveness. Understanding Ivana's motives might help to ease your pain."

Elliot remained silent for a moment while he considered her words, and then he nodded, his shoulders sagging as he surrendered. "I will not disappoint you. I will do what you ask. I will be the man you want me to be."

"You're already that man." Despite her reservations, she pulled back the sheet and straddled his naked body. She gave a coy smile, knowing what he needed to help soothe his spirit. "Perhaps you could show me again how much I mean to you."

His mouth curved up into a wicked grin. "It will be my pleasure."

CHAPTER 13

*A*s soon as Ivana's carriage rattled over the castle's cobblestone bridge, her solemn mood improved. Just knowing she would spend the night encased in Leo's strong arms was enough to chase away all morbid thoughts of the children and the Bruhns.

Leo rushed to meet her in the courtyard. His shirt was untucked from his breeches, open at the neck to reveal bronze skin and a dusting of dark hair. His sinful brown eyes devoured her. She drank in the splendid sight knowing she had but a day or two left with him. Her heart sang only to his tune; her soul yearned for his touch. After years of fighting her feelings, years pretending she felt nothing, she wanted to release the trapped emotions, to give life to the words she longed to say.

She ran to him, threw herself into his arms, and kissed him frantically as she clawed at his muscular body. "I love you," she whispered. "I have always loved you."

It didn't matter that he did not declare his feelings. There were huge gaps in his memory. She sensed his confusion, knew his heart was racked with guilt for betraying his friends.

Desire burst forth. The need to sate their ravaging hunger took hold.

He scooped her up into his arms, kicked the wooden door open with his boot. "I need you," he growled. "I need you now."

Leo held her tight to his chest as he marched through the corridors and up the curling stone staircase. She knew his eagerness to join with her also stemmed from a need to suppress all sombre thoughts. As soon as he set her down near the bed, they were tearing at clothes, stripping away layers, desperate for the comforting touch of warm skin.

"Make me remember," he whispered as he sucked on the soft fleshy lobe of her ear, rained kisses down the column of her throat.

"Let us not think of the past anymore," she replied breathlessly. They could not look to the future, either. "We will think only of this moment. We will make a new memory, one that will never be forgotten."

Their last coupling had been urgent, fast and frenzied. They had drunk each other's blood until their bodies tingled and thrummed. They had cried loud and long during their release.

"Wait," she muttered as he covered her naked body and pressed her down into the plush mattress. "I want to savour this moment, Leo. I want you to imagine this is the last time we will be together."

Ivana did not have to imagine. This would be their last time. The memory would have to last her for a lifetime.

He propped himself up on one elbow, caressed her cheek with the palm of his hand. "You want it slow," he said in the languid drawl that made her core pulse. "You want to feel every movement when I fill you."

"Yes." The word drifted through the room as though carried on a gentle breeze.

Sporting a wicked grin, he trailed the tips of his fingers along her collarbone, down the valley between her breasts. When he brushed lightly back and forth over her nipple, she arched her back as the sweet spot between her legs throbbed.

A soft moan escaped from her lips.

As he continued to stroke and tease her, she realised it was not what she needed. It was not pleasure she sought. She needed to feel at one with him. "I want to join with you. I don't want to wait."

Without needing any other prompt he nudged her legs apart, settled between her thighs and pushed home. Her soul sang in celebration. She hugged him tight, clamped around the solid length never wanting to let him go. With each measured thrust he filled her full. The sensation caused waves of pleasure, waves of pure love to ripple through her body.

His heated gaze locked with hers. "Is this what you want, Ivana?" The words caressed her, the slow rhythmical rocking creating a more intimate, more emotional coupling.

"I … I want you, Leo. For now … for always."

She drank in the sight of his full lips, parting with a groan as she drew him deeper. She memorised the golden flecks in his brown eyes, how they twinkled when glazed with desire. She inhaled his earthy masculine scent, let it surround her and seep into her skin.

They were as one—one body, one heart, one soul.

Nothing else mattered.

Feeling a sudden urge to claim him, to heighten his pleasure, she wrapped her legs tightly around his thighs and forced him to flip over. Straddling him whilst he sat up, she pressed her body close until her breasts were squashed against his chest. She rolled her hips, ground against him, the movement causing him to moan against her neck as he sucked and nipped the sensitive skin.

"God, Ivana, I can never get enough of you."

She wrapped her arms around his neck and claimed his mouth. Each thrust of her tongue mimicked the movement of the most adept part of his anatomy. The temptation to rush almost overwhelmed her, but she maintained the pace. Strong hands settled on her buttocks to massage the soft flesh, to assist with each delicious slide.

If only they could spend every night like this. If only she could spend an eternity joined with him. Love caused her heart to swell; love caused the blood to pool hot and heavy between her legs. Love caused the tears to form, caused the pain in her throat.

Ivana kissed him one last time, licked his lips, tasted the essence of her one true mate. "Look at me, Leo." She could feel the light pulling her forward. Soon she would be riding high on a wave of ecstasy.

Beneath hooded lids, he gazed into her eyes. "I'll never leave you," he groaned as his movements grew more frantic.

"Know that I ... I will be with you always."

"Oh, God." His head fell back, and he closed his eyes. "This is heaven."

"Look at me," she whispered, contracting the muscles in her core.

He obeyed. They stared at each other, their silent communication revealing all they felt in their hearts. Their release burst brightly, a glittering shower of pure love raining down upon them. If she lived a thousand lifetimes, no other man would ever make her feel so complete.

Ivana groaned when he withdrew, the sensation reminding her they must soon part. They collapsed on the bed, and he pulled her into an embrace. Ivana put her head on his chest to listen to the rhythmical sound of his breathing. The dusting of dark hair tickled her cheek, and she inhaled deeply as his intoxicating masculine scent enveloped her. If she spent the rest of her days in the fiery pits of Hell, this moment would be enough to sustain her.

She closed her eyes to join him in feigned slumber. Sleep was a pleasure long since denied them. With her mind relaxed and body sated she could forget all about her troubles. In the blissful state, it was easy to imagine how wonderful it would be to spend every day in his arms.

Ivana.

Her name drifted into her thoughts, and she wondered if Leo had called out to her.

I am home, Ivana. I have returned to you.

The words hit her like the sudden slash of a whip: hard, quick, the sharp pain causing her to jump up from the bed.

"No!" she cried, unable to suppress the depths of her despair. "It can't be true. Not now. Not yet."

Leo opened his eyes with a start. "What … what is it?"

Naked, she scampered from the bed and raced over to the window, pushing her nose to the pane. Narrowing her gaze, she stared out into the night. The light from the full moon cut through the mist to cast an eerie silver sheen over the tree-tops. But she did not have to see anything to know that the Devil was nearing her door. The rattling of carriage wheels echoed through the valley, the sound a menacing warning of evil approaching.

She swung around to face Leo, knowing her countenance reflected the horror about to unfold. "Quick. Quick. You must leave." She could barely speak, barely breathe. "You must leave now and take your friends far away from this place."

With a frown marring his handsome brow, Leo came to

stand at her side, peered through the window at the carriage rumbling towards the bridge. "What is it, Ivana?"

"He has come home, Leo." She fell to the floor in a terrified heap, the muscles in her legs no longer able to support her weight.

"Who, Ivana?" Leo pulled her up and held her tight, stroked her hair, but nothing could help soothe her fears now. "It is Nikolai. He has come home. You must leave. You must go now."

"Who is he, Ivana?"

A sob burst from her lips. "Nikolai is my husband."

CHAPTER 14

"Your husband!" Leo shook his head. He should have been shocked, utterly dumbfounded. But he had always known there was a missing piece of the puzzle, another missing memory waiting to be discovered.

Ivana tugged at his arm. "Please, Leo. You must go. He cannot find you here again."

"Again?"

"He will not let you live this time." She clasped his face roughly between her palms, kissed him ten times or more in quick succession. His cheek felt damp from her tears. "Go. You must leave before it is too late." She ran her hands over the muscles in his chest before pushing him back towards the door. "I love you."

Leo stood and watched her thrust her arms into her robe, fumble with the rope ties, and straighten the sheets on the bed.

How could she expect him to leave after all that had happened between them? He had come to Bavaria expecting to die. To him, death was by far the most preferable option to spending a life alone.

"I'm not leaving."

Ivana swung around, barely able to catch her breath. "Do not make me compel you to go. I will force you if I must."

He marched over to her, his strides long and purposeful. "Then we will have a battle on our hands. You cannot expect me to forget all of this." He waved his hand over the bed as he struggled to find adequate words to convey what they had shared. It went beyond the physical realm. It went beyond anything he could comprehend. "You cannot think I could walk away."

"You must," she implored. "Nikolai has borne the affliction for too long. He is stronger and more powerful than either of us."

So Nikolai was the one responsible for turning her.

"Do you still care for him?" Leo narrowed his gaze. He struggled to form the next question though he knew he had to ask. "Do you love him, too?"

Ivana's hand flew to her chest, and she took a step back. "Good heavens, no! I have never loved him. I have not seen him since the day you left three years ago. Before that, he has stayed here only a handful of times."

What sort of husband lived separately from his wife?

"Then where has he been all this time?"

"I don't know."

Conscious of the look of panic etched on her face he asked, "I do not know the penalty for adultery in Bavaria, but is that what you fear?"

Ivana snorted. "Nikolai does not care about silly things like that. I mean nothing to him."

Leo's head felt heavy, weighed down with the burden of so many unanswered questions, so many overwhelming emotions. There were too many things to consider: her fears for Herr Bruhn and the children, his friendship with Elliot and Alexander, the depth of his affection for Ivana.

And now her husband had returned.

Ivana placed her palms on his chest. "If you care for me at all, then you must go."

Leo was guilty of many things, but he was not a coward. "Tell me why? Why must I leave? Why can we not discuss the matter with him?"

"Because I cannot live in a world without you in it. Because I do not want you to die."

"You want me to leave for selfish reasons?" Leo knew he had to be blunt if he had any hope of persuading her otherwise.

Her eyes grew wide. "Selfish? It is not selfish to want to save another's life. It is not selfish to protect those you love."

"It is selfish to go against a person's wishes just to ease your pain and guilt."

She swallowed visibly, opened her mouth and snapped it shut.

"I came here for revenge," he continued. "If I'm to understand you correctly, Nikolai threatened to kill me once before, which is part of the reason you wiped my memory and forced me to leave. I was weak then, not so now."

She rushed to the window and peered out. "You are not as strong as Nikolai."

"Together we may have a chance against him." Leo marched over to her, pulled her from the window and held her face between his hands. "I would rather die trying to save what we have here than live a life unloved and unfulfilled."

She closed her eyes as her head fell forward to rest on his chest. "You make it sound so simple."

"It is simple." He stroked her hair to soothe her. "We share a soul-deep connection. The overwhelming ache I have for you in my chest will not be tempered. No other woman will ever be good enough for me. It is you, or it is no one."

She looked up at him; fear flashed in her eyes. "He will kill us both."

"Perhaps, but it is a chance we must take. We are stronger if we work together."

Ivana gasped. "He does not know about Elliot and Alexander. He does not know I poisoned their blood. He would have killed them if he'd known."

Leo smiled. "Then we have an advantage. If needs must, I will call them to assist us."

Ivana stepped back, clasped her hands under her chin as though in prayer. "Do you think they would come after everything I have done?"

Leo searched his heart for the answer as opposed to his head. "I would trust them with my life. I am confident they would come if I called."

Her countenance brightened. "Do you think we have the strength to overthrow him?"

"We can but try, Ivana." They had too much to lose to fail.

She nodded apprehensively. "The choice is yours. I do not care what happens to me. I will concede to your wishes. I will do whatever you ask."

"Then we should dress and meet your husband in the Great Hall."

"You must not call out to your friends in his presence. He will feel and hear the emotional connection you share. You must write a note, and I will ask Julia to take it to the tavern. Quick. We must hurry."

CHAPTER 15

They entered the Great Hall to find Nikolai lounging in a chair by the fire. His legs were stretched out in front of him, his hands cupping the back of his head. Upon hearing their approaching footsteps, he glanced in their direction and smirked.

"Ivana, there you are."

Leo could feel Ivana trembling at his side.

Nikolai stood. He turned to face them as he clasped his hands behind his back. His silky black hair touched his shoulders. With him being both tall and lithe, his features were well defined. Possessing a thin patrician nose, prominent chin, and sunken cheeks, he had an air of hauteur. His black velvet coat trimmed with gold brocade reflected a fashion popular forty years earlier. Leo knew the silver cane propped against the chair sheathed a sword because Calvino owned one similar.

"Ah, Leo, what a surprise it is to see you again."

Sylvester stepped forward carrying another chair which he placed next to the fire. He lit the candelabras before trudging out of the room.

"I'm afraid you have an advantage," Leo said with a hint of contempt. "I cannot recall ever meeting you. I remember almost nothing of my time here."

Nikolai raised an arrogant brow. "If that is the case, then pray tell me how you knew where to come."

The gentleman was sharp.

"Not all memories were lost to me. I knew to come to the tavern if I had any hope of finding and killing the woman who turned me. I came here for revenge."

Nikolai laughed and glanced at Ivana. "How interesting. Obviously, you were unsuccessful in your task." He inhaled deeply. "Indeed, I sense some other need drives you now."

"What are you doing here?" There was a nervous edge to Ivana's tone.

Nikolai jerked his head, looked a little confused. "This is my home, Ivana, or had you forgotten that too?" He gestured to the chairs. "Let us talk for a while."

Like any good host, Nikolai waited for them to sit before dropping into a chair.

"I had not forgotten," Ivana retorted. "But it is a home you have spent no more than a week in since we married."

"Ah, so you did remember our vows when you took your friend here to your bed."

Leo sat forward. He was tired of playing games, tired of skirting around the truth. "What do you want with Ivana? Why have you come back?"

Ivana sucked in a breath. "Forgive Leo." She waved her hands nervously. "He does not know what he is saying. He is a little overwrought. That is all."

"Do not speak for me, Ivana." Anger infused Leo's tone as he refused to let Nikolai see him as weak. "I am not a child."

Nikolai's eyes grew wide with amusement. "What is this?

A lovers' tiff? How quaint." In the blink of an eye, his expression darkened. "Not that it is any business of yours, but I have come home to reclaim what is mine."

Ivana gripped the arms of the chair. "What do you mean?"

"Have no fear, I am not talking about you, Ivana. You have served your purpose. After tonight, I no longer need you to keep watch for me here."

Ivana gulped down a breath as she tried to speak. "You … you mean to lift the spell so I can leave."

"No," Nikolai said with a smirk. He picked up the cane and rolled the stem between his fingers. "I have no intention of lifting the spell."

Leo watched the hope in her eyes fade. "What spell?"

"I cannot leave the village," she explained. "I cannot travel more than a few miles, ten at most. Nikolai compelled me to stay."

"Why?"

Ivana shrugged. "He will not tell me."

Nikolai placed the cane across his legs, one hand gripping it tight. "I will tell you whatever you want to know. All you need do is ask."

Rather than look appeased by the offer, Ivana's face turned pale, ashen. "You mean to kill us both," she gasped as her eyes grew round and wide. "You would not divulge information and then let us live."

"You were never slow-witted, Ivana. I mean to leave nothing here that would cause me any problems in the future," Nikolai said coldly.

Leo contemplated punching him until his knuckles bled, until Nikolai's face was unrecognisable. But he sensed he would have to be far more subtle, far shrewder in his approach if they were to survive.

"If we are to die," he said, turning to Ivana, "ask him anything you want to know."

Leo hated seeing terror taint her pretty blue eyes. He wanted to tell her not to worry, but Nikolai would hear his words and he did not wish to give him access to his thoughts.

"He lies," Ivana protested. "He will not tell me anything."

Nikolai smirked. "I will answer any question put to me. Call it a token of my gratitude for acting as the guardian of this abode."

Ivana raised her chin. "Why … why did you marry me when you had no intention of living with me?"

"It is simple. I needed money to further my cause at home, and your parents were wealthy, easy to compel. Indeed, they proved to be rather generous in the end. I will not deny that when I saw you in Vienna, I wanted to have you." He waved his hand at her, the frilly cuffs of his shirt flapping at the end of his coat sleeves. "But you know my heart is empty when it comes to things other than war, other than taking back what I believe is rightfully mine."

The man talked in riddles.

"Then it is as I suspected," she said, bitterness dripping from every word. "You used me for your own gain. Out of greed and spite, you turned me into the monster you see before you."

"We are not monsters," he replied indignantly. "We are strong, powerful creatures who cannot be easily manipulated by others. My affliction has helped me gain back my lands."

"You manipulated me."

"Yes. But only because I needed to keep you here."

Ivana shot out of the chair. "Why?"

Nikolai tutted. "For this reason." He waved his hand over her again. "You are too impetuous, too needy. You think with your heart and not your head. I do not need such a distraction."

Leo sat in silence and watched the exchange. Nikolai was not being entirely honest with them. During their conversation, while Nikolai focused on answering Ivana's questions, Leo attempted to pick up threads of his thoughts. Nikolai had come back for something, something of great value. It had nothing to do with Ivana. It was an object, an item of extreme importance.

Nikolai glanced at him suspiciously, and so Leo sought to ask a question of his own to distract him further. "Is it your intention to remain at the castle?"

Nikolai examined his fingernails. "I'm afraid it will be uninhabitable after the fire."

"Fire! What fire?" Ivana flopped down in the chair, her frantic gaze locking with his. Despite her husband sitting a few feet away, Leo took her hand and caressed it with his thumb.

Nikolai's flippant comment revealed another clue: the item he wanted could be found within the stone walls.

Sylvester's discreet cough drew their attention. He hovered behind them waiting for permission to step forward. Nikolai waved for him to come closer. Noticing the vials of burgundy liquid lying on the silver tray he gave a disdainful snort.

"I have already fed this evening, on a delightful wench in a town not too far from here." He picked at his teeth, examined his fingers. "I do so hate it when they struggle. There is a tendency to overindulge."

Sylvester presented Ivana with the tray.

"Please tell me, you are not still drinking animal blood?" Nikolai continued.

Ivana opened her mouth to answer, but Leo spoke first. "Tonight we will follow your lead." He waved the tray away, turned to Ivana and smiled as a way to reassure her. "Tonight we will drink from each other in celebration of our last night together. That is if your husband has no objection."

"I would not deny you the opportunity to take one last meal."

Nikolai's expression revealed his indifference. If he had no feelings for Ivana why had he forced Leo to leave once before? Why had he threatened to kill him? Logic told him it must stem from a need to protect the mysterious object.

Leo pulled Ivana to her feet. She tilted her head to give him free access to the vein.

The sight of her elegant neck coupled with the thought of tasting her blood caused desire to flare. "Trust me." He whispered the words as his fangs burst from their sheath, piercing the vein with ease.

She grew limp in his arms while he drank. He could feel her life force flowing through him, energising, strengthening, just as he'd hoped. If they were going to fight Nikolai, they would need to be strong.

A soft moan escaped from her lips. Her husband shuffled in his chair and cleared his throat. It would not do to rouse his ire at this point, and so Leo pulled away, licked the residue from the white tips.

Leo tugged at the collar of his shirt, encouraged Ivana to feed. "Take what you need."

The moment she drew his blood, his cock twitched. An image of their erotic coupling entered his mind, and he dismissed it for fear the sensation would cloud his ability to focus.

"Enough." Nikolai's voice echoed through the Great Hall.

Ivana straightened. She dabbed at the corners of her mouth, a deep look of longing evident as she raised her hand to caress Leo's cheek. "I will always love you."

Leo blinked rapidly, surprised she had given a voice to her feelings in the presence of her husband. All the things he wanted to say were lost under the pressure of Nikolai's intense glare.

"Sentiment is for the weak." Nikolai flicked a speck from his coat. "It is for those who fear loneliness. It is for those who lack the courage to feed naturally."

"There is nothing natural about our affliction," Ivana spat. She moved to Leo's side and hugged his arm. "It is a grotesque mutation of all that is good."

Nikolai snorted. "Well, I for one will miss the sense of detachment that comes when one drinks from the host. I find human emotions far more debilitating, but it is something I must conquer if I am to keep my lands and the respect of my people."

Still feeling lightheaded from taking Ivana's blood, Leo tried to make sense of the cryptic comment. "You make it sound as though you have a choice."

"Oh, I do." Nikolai chuckled though his mouth hardly twitched and his eyes were cold and black. "I suppose it will not hurt to boast of my ingenious plan as come the morning you will both be dead."

Ivana clutched his arm tight. Leo refused to be intimidated but did not refute Nikolai's claim as he was eager to discover the reason for his return.

"Do not listen to him," Ivana said, revealing her contempt. "He is playing games with us."

"Now you know that is not true, Ivana."

"Why must you kill us?" Leo would keep him talking in a

bid to delay his inevitable attack. "If you no longer need Ivana, then let us go."

"I cannot. You know too much." He waved to the chairs, but they refused to sit. "You will seek revenge, reveal my secret. When I am human, you will be stronger, easily able to kill me."

"Human?" Ivana jerked back. "You have lost your mind. Why do you taunt us with your lies?"

"They are not lies, Ivana. It is just that you do not remember. I have taken the cure before. You were the one who bit me again so I could become strong. So you see, you did have a purpose."

"The cure?" they both cried in unison.

A hundred questions raced through Leo's mind. Was this just another attempt to weaken their resolve? If there was a cure why didn't Ivana know of it? How was such a thing even possible? Their blood contained poison; their skin could no longer withstand sunlight.

"Indeed, I must take it again. My people are suspicious by nature. They believe in witchcraft, omens, and signs. There are whispers that I collude with the Devil. That I sold my soul for the power to overthrow my brother. I must be seen to walk in the sun to secure their loyalty. So, I will return to my human form, marry and bear sons to continue my legacy."

Leo understood his motive now. "And so you plan to destroy any evidence before you leave here."

Nikolai nodded as he steepled his fingers. "Yes. There will be a terrible fire, everything but Talliano's notes and the cure will be lost."

"Talliano?"

"He was a friend, a man of wisdom and great knowledge. I'm afraid he is dead now and was kind enough to leave me the castle in his will."

Leo suspected the only reason Talliano was dead was because Nikolai had killed him.

"It will be a shame to destroy such an old building." Nikolai looked up at the vaulted ceiling. "Of course, you know Sylvester and Julia must perish too."

"No!" Ivana threw herself to the floor, knelt at his feet. "Do not do this, Nikolai. They have been loyal servants to me all these years. You can make us forget. Take what it is you want and leave us be. Do the vows you made to me mean nothing to you?"

"As I said, did you remember your vows when you took Leo to your bed?" Nikolai grinned. "But as this is the last time I will see you, it may ease your conscience to know that you are not my wife. I have married many women over the years, in many countries. You were not the first. You were not the last."

Relief flooded Leo's chest. If Nikolai was not her husband, then he had no real hold on Ivana.

"What?" Ivana shook her head. "You mean mine is not the only life you have destroyed out of greed and a need for revenge. Your heart is black. Your wickedness taints your soul. May God damn you to Hell."

"Yes, yes. I have heard it all before." He grabbed his cane and stood as Ivana scrambled to her feet and shuffled back to Leo's side. "Now, I must leave here within the hour. Forgive my impatience but time is of the essence."

The sharp slicing sound of the blade as it came free of its holder echoed ominously through the room.

Ivana raised her chin defiantly though Leo could sense her fear. "I will not let you do this."

"You always were naive. But you will watch your lover die and know that you were to blame. Your eagerness to turn him has cost him his life." Nikolai grinned in response to the tears welling in her eyes. "The blood of animals has made you weak."

"The blood of humans has made you a monster," she countered.

Nikolai shrugged, but then turned sharply, his penetrative gaze boring into Leo's soul. "Kneel before me, Leo. You will kneel before me now." Nikolai's stern voice gripped him like talons, puncturing his chest to curl around his heart. It tugged, pulled him forward. Leo tried desperately to hold on to the arm of the chair, but his legs had a will of their own. "Do not fight me. You will kneel before me."

You must fight him.

Ivana rushed forward and yanked on his arm. "Stop, Leo. You will step back. You will listen to me."

Nikolai snorted. "I do not need him to kneel. But perhaps you should be the first to lose your head. Disloyalty is a crime punishable by death in my country. Kneel, kneel before me, Ivana."

Leo watched her struggle, the pain on her face evident as the vice-like grip around his body disappeared. "You must fight him, Ivana."

"I cannot." Ivana tumbled to her knees as Nikolai stepped forward.

Anger burst forth, forcing Leo's fangs from their sheath. He darted forward, but Nikolai raised his hand, an invisible barrier bringing Leo to an abrupt halt. "You will not kill her," he repeated over and over again. "Step away, Nikolai."

"Step away," Ivana repeated weakly but then regained her confidence. "Step away."

Nikolai faltered but only for a few seconds. "You are too weak to stop me."

"Do not surrender, Ivana. We must fight him together."

Nikolai threw his head back and laughed. "I am too

strong. It will take more than two feeble minds to prevent me from achieving my goal."

The thud of booted footsteps captured their attention.

"How about four feeble minds?" Elliot's arrogant tone brought instant relief. "What say you, Alexander? Do you think we should show the gentleman our teeth?"

CHAPTER 16

$\mathcal{N}$ikolai stared at Elliot and froze, his look of supreme confidence replaced with one of subdued enquiry.

"Step away," Elliot roared. Years of strutting around the ballrooms of London had given him an air of arrogance and conceit. His commanding presence roused a flicker of uncertainty in Nikolai's beady black eyes. "Put your sword on the floor and step away."

Leo put his arm around Ivana and helped her to her feet, pulling her back to a safe distance for fear Nikolai would lash out in a sudden fit of temper. As his brothers came to stand behind them, he caught Elliot's gaze and gave a look that conveyed his gratitude for their timely assistance.

As two, they would struggle to overpower Nikolai.

As four, they stood a much greater chance.

Strength came in the form of loyal friendships forged during times of hardship. It came from knowing others loved you enough to sacrifice their own happiness to stand at your side. It came from the realisation that, despite all thoughts to the contrary, you were not alone.

A smirk touched the corners of Nikolai's mouth as his gaze drifted over them. "My, you have been busy, Ivana. I have underestimated your skill in combat it seems. You have amassed an army of night creatures to do your bidding."

"We are not creatures." Leo squared his shoulders as his lips curled down in disdain. "We are brothers. We are men willing to stand together for what we believe in. Now you will put your sword on the floor as instructed."

Nikolai's expression remained impassive. When he surrendered his weapon, he showed no sign it was because he had been compelled to do so.

"Kick the sword away," Elliot commanded, and Nikolai obliged without question.

Nikolai tugged at the ends of his coat sleeves. "What is it you want?"

Ivana turned and looked at Leo. An hour earlier, he would have been happy for Nikolai to walk away. But he knew they could not trust him. Should Nikolai escape, he would return. He would kill them all one by one. He would seek retribution.

Nonetheless, one thought took precedence and refused to be tempered. Nikolai knew of an answer to all of their prayers. "There is only one thing you have that interests us."

Nikolai narrowed his gaze. "You speak of the cure. You wish for an end to your nightmare."

He heard his brothers gasp, could sense their shock and disbelief. "We will all take the cure together." Leo's heart soared at the thought that there could be a tonic or a pill to swallow that would eradicate all the horrendous effects of their affliction. "Only then will we all be equal men. Only then will we let you leave here."

A heavy silence permeated the air.

"That is not an option," Nikolai said with a sinister

chuckle. "I will not surrender the cure. Not under any circumstances. You will have to kill me. If you think you can."

"I knew it was all a lie." Ivana threw her arms up, her anger evident in her venomous tone. "He finds amusement in other people's misery. He gives hope when he knows there is none."

But Nikolai had returned for something important, something worth killing for. Hope blossomed in Leo's chest. To feel the sun warm his face again would be a dream he had never believed possible.

"Perhaps you could be persuaded." Leo kept his voice calm for fear of revealing a hint of desperation.

What if they combined their efforts and compelled Nikolai to do their bidding? But to do so, would give him open access to their thoughts. There was a chance Nikolai would manipulate one of them, force a mutiny amongst ranks.

Nikolai dropped into the chair with languid grace. "Of course, I am willing to fight for the right to leave, fight to the death if necessary. If you win, you would have access to the cure."

The temptation to accept was great indeed.

"You think you are a match for all of us?" Leo asked incredulously though he suspected Nikolai knew a way to even the odds.

"No, Leo," he replied with a smirk as he folded his arms across his chest. "I think I am a match for you. As a gentleman, it is a question of honour. This is my home, and you have come here and taken something that belongs to me—"

"I belong to no man," Ivana yelled.

"There is a debt to be paid," Nikolai said in an amused tone. "To refuse would mean you deem Ivana unworthy. To refuse would mean you are a coward."

Damn him! The man was a master of manipulation.

Leo's respect for Ivana, his pride, and years of aristocratic breeding forced him to accept. "It would need to be a fair fight. It—"

"No!" Ivana turned to him, gripped his arms and made him look at her. "It is a trick. He will kill you and then we will be too weak in our grief to stop him. Let us just kill him now and be done with it."

Leo doubted it would be so simple. He shook his head, glanced at his brothers' solemn expressions. "It is a matter of integrity, Ivana. Nikolai has laid down the challenge, and I must accept. I must fight for you. I must fight for us."

"No. I won't let you. Do you hear me?" She thumped his chest with her clenched fists, the sound like a hollow drum. "I don't want you. I lied when I said I loved you." She fell to her knees, wrapped her arms around his leg and hugged it tight as she sobbed.

Leo glanced back over his shoulder. He locked gazes with Alexander, who came towards them and helped Ivana to her feet. "You are certain this is what you want to do?" Alexander said as he held Ivana to his chest.

"It is the only way. Would you not do the same in my situation?"

Showing some reluctance, Alexander nodded.

Elliot stepped closer and placed his hand on Leo's shoulder. "After all that has happened, I cannot lose your friendship now. But I understand your desire to do what is right, what is needed." He sighed deeply. "Forgive me, for the way I acted earlier. Know that I will never fail you again."

"There is nothing to forgive. You have been my constant companion these last few years and during all that time you have always had my best interests at heart."

"All this sentimental talk makes me feel nauseous,"

Nikolai complained. "Well, are you man enough to accept the challenge, Leo?"

Leo's mouth curled into an arrogant grin. "I think you know the answer."

Leo did not wish to reveal his preferred method of engagement, but he suspected from Nikolai's dress and cane that a sword would be his weapon of choice. Or, at least, he hoped that was the case. Besides, a fight to the death meant one of them must lose their head. Hence, a blade was a necessity. "Are we to fight in hand-to-hand combat?" he said, feigning ignorance.

Nikolai sneered. "There is something so unrefined, something so vulgar about using one's fists."

"If we are to duel, I doubt you will find someone to act as your second."

"A pistol is the weapon of a coward. There is little skill involved, and I am not a man who gambles his life on the efficiency of a trigger. We will fight as our ancestors did. We will fight with swords."

Leo grinned inwardly. He would soon discover if Calvino's tutoring had been worth the extortionate price he had paid. "As you have chosen the weapon, I feel it only fair I should choose the place."

Nikolai rose from the chair and gave a dandified wave. "As you wish."

Spatial awareness was the key to winning any fight. Leo knew he must choose an environment that worked to his advantage. His tuition had taken place in an empty room. Calvino believed one must not rely on barriers or objects as a means of defence. To hide behind a chair or table only served to weaken the mind: it gave a false sense of security. A swordsman must possess the skill necessary to defend in the dark. He should not need to see his opponent to anticipate his movements.

"I choose the courtyard."

Nikolai appeared surprised.

Elliot bent his head and whispered, "It is raining. The cobblestones will be slippery underfoot."

Leo suppressed a grin. "I know."

The terrain must never be a disadvantage.

Calvino's words drifted through his mind as he recalled the time he had ridiculed his teacher for forcing him to parry whilst standing in a pit filled with small lead balls.

Ivana looked up at him. "Please, Leo. We will find some other way. If you care for me at all, please do not do this."

Leo cupped her cheek, wiped a tear away with the pad of his thumb. "I love you, Ivana." He felt the truth of it as the words left his lips. "But there is no other option open to us. I will not take a man's life when he is outnumbered. To do so, would make me a coward, a murderer."

"But he wants to kill you."

"Yes. And I will defend myself when necessary."

She clutched his shirt. "I can't watch you die."

"Have a little faith," he said, knowing that all of their lives depended upon the outcome of this battle. "But know that whatever happens, I believe death brings peace. It brings freedom from our affliction."

"Don't say that." She wrapped her arms around him. "Don't leave me again."

Leo could feel sorrow's empty cavern opening up in his chest. Such an emotional exchange was not the best way to prepare for combat. He nodded to Elliot, who understood his concern without him needing to say a word.

"Come, Ivana," Elliot said, taking her by her arms and guiding her away. "We must let him prepare."

Calvino's methods were influenced by many philosophies from the ancient world. A warrior must embrace battle not fear it. The mind must be calm, focused, the body relaxed. In combat, one must follow a code of honour. Leo had an unusually long reach, which had served him well on many occasions. He suspected Nikolai would use any tactic necessary to win. And so, he would need to be prepared to do the same.

"There are many swords littered about the walls of the castle," Nikolai said. "You may take any one of them."

"That will not be necessary. I have my own sword." Leo noted the faint flicker of surprise in the blackguard's eyes. Indeed, Leo's sword was an extension of himself. It felt comfortable, almost weightless in his hand.

Nikolai inclined his head. "Then I shall meet you in the courtyard."

Just like the night he challenged Ivana outside Herr Bruhn's house, the rain lashed against the castle's facade, bounced off the cobblestones, hammered on the rooftops. Leo glanced at the puddles, noting their number, estimating their depth. He stood in the centre, closed his eyes briefly in order to feel at one with his surroundings.

Nikolai stood opposite him. Without his fancy coat, he appeared less menacing and so twirled his sword in a figure of eight as a means to intimidate. Leo ignored the slicing sound, the way the blade whipped at the air. The vigorous movements would only serve to tire him, and the thought gave Leo a little more confidence in his ability to succeed.

Elliot, Alexander, and Ivana stood near the large oak door. Despite Elliot's initial anger over his relationship with Ivana, his friend held her close to his chest, rubbed her arm to offer comfort. Sylvester and Julia joined them, and Leo wondered if they were aware their own lives hinged on the outcome of this fight.

Leo's heart swelled with love for his friends, and for the only woman he had ever truly wanted. But he knew he must detach from all feelings of sentimentality if he had any hope of beating Nikolai. The mind was a fragile thing. Calvino once told him that armour was worn not just as a means of protection, but as a way to sever emotional ties. Dress a beggar in the clothes of a prince and he will behave with more decorum. A suit of steel worked to harden the heart and Leo imagined donning a vest of chain mail for the same reason.

Nikolai stopped his twirling and flexed his fingers before firming his grip on the hilt. "Are you ready?"

Are you ready to die?

Nikolai's voice permeated his thoughts, and he batted it away as though it were nought but an annoying little fly.

Wearing an arrogant grin, Nikolai stepped forward, his linen shirt sodden as it clung to his lithe frame.

Leo inhaled deeply, blinked away the rivulets of rain clinging to his lashes. He held his sword in front of him, the tip pointing at Nikolai's throat, and waited for him to attack.

Nikolai swung first, the movement controlled as their blades clashed. The sound of meeting metal vibrated through the air like the crack of a thunderbolt hurled down by the gods. Leo defended the first flurry of attacks. It gave him an opportunity to gauge Nikolai's experience. As suspected, the man had skill, but his movements were predictable.

The majority of sword fights lasted no more than thirty seconds. Leo followed the set routine, a sequence of moves intended to lure one's opponent into making his first error. With Leo's speed, he managed to avert an attack, his long reach catching his opponent by surprise as the tip of his blade scratched Nikolai's jaw.

The sight of the thin sliver of blood bolstered Leo's confidence. But he knew he had to remain calm and composed. There was a natural flow in all things. One must find and settle into the pace, for to fight against the current only serves to drain one's strength.

"So you think you know how to handle a blade." Nikolai's condescending tone did not distract him.

"It's been said I am the finest swordsman in England." It was not his intention to boast but to chip away at Nikolai's confidence.

Of course, he came back at him with a comment as disabling as the most vicious blow. "When I've killed you, Leo, know that I shall take pleasure in torturing Ivana. You will hear her screams from the pits of Hell."

Ivana gasped.

Nikolai had found the chink in his armour. A host of terrifying images flashed through his mind. Ivana would always be his weakness, and he found his gaze drawn to her if only for a fraction of a second.

It was enough to give Nikolai an advantage. Underestimating the force of his opponent's offensive, Leo stumbled, losing his balance on the wet stones as he defended against another barrage of attacks.

Ivana's ear-piercing cry only served to divert his attention further.

As he tumbled back, his sword flew from his hand, was sent skittering across the courtyard and out of reach. Nikolai charged at him, flashed a devilish grin as he raised his sword to deliver the final fatal blow. But Nikolai was reckless in his eagerness to win. Over-confidence was a weakness too. In an attempt to dodge the attack, Leo rolled on to his side. He continued rolling until he came within an inch of his sword. As his hand curled around the hilt, he turned and thrust sharply, the point of his blade almost touching the hard lump in Nikolai's throat as the man towered over him holding his sword aloft.

"Surrender your weapon," Leo commanded. "You will surrender your weapon now."

"Never! Your mind manipulation will not work on me." Nikolai narrowed his gaze, his black eyes showing no fear. "You will lower your sword." Nikolai's firm command caused Leo's arm to tremble. "You will do as I say. You will lower your sword."

Be strong, Leo.

Elliot's words invaded his thoughts, but Nikolai's words were like thick vines creeping through his body to strangle his limbs.

Please, Leo, you must fight it.

Ivana's plea only served to weaken his resolve.

"Lower your sword," Nikolai repeated.

Leo's arm had a will of its own and he heard Ivana scream when the weapon fell from his grasp.

Nikolai smiled. "Did you think I would let you win? Abiding by your gentlemanly code of honour was your downfall. You should have pooled your resources. You should have bared your fangs. You should have turned into the creatures you detest. Yes, one or two of you would have died, but it was the only way for you to have your victory."

Lying on the cobblestones, Leo glanced at his friends expecting to see fear and terror in their eyes. But Elliot's calm countenance surprised him.

"Say goodbye, Leo." Nikolai sneered. "I may even take Ivana to my bed before I put her out of her misery."

Anger flared in Leo's chest. With his hand near a puddle,

he flicked the water, splashing Nikolai in the eyes. It was as though time slowed. Nikolai blinked and sputtered as he raised his sword a few inches above his head to gain more momentum. Ivana fell to her knees with her hands clasped in prayer.

"Roll to the left, Leo," Elliot shouted just as the tip of an iron spear burst through Nikolai's chest.

Leo rolled away as Nikolai's eyes grew wide with shock, his mouth falling open as he gasped for breath. He stumbled forward, the weight of his sword suddenly becoming a heavy burden.

"I've never been one for gentlemanly conduct," Sylvester said as he pushed Nikolai to the floor and twisted the spear further into his back. He bent down and picked up Leo's sword. "I've got no patience for men who threaten women, either."

As Nikolai groaned and cried out in his mother tongue, Sylvester grabbed him by the hair and with one mighty swing banished the devil from their door for good.

CHAPTER 17

*I*vana stared at Nikolai's body lying on the wet cobblestones.

A sudden sense of relief obliterated the fear that had been her constant companion for many years. Any memories lost to her by Nikolai's hand sprung to life in her mind like fresh buds unfurling in spring. She remembered it all. She remembered everything.

Nikolai had not lied.

There was a cure. It lay hidden somewhere in the dark depths of the castle though he had never told her where. Despite her burning curiosity, she shook her head to clear her thoughts before fanciful notions of being human again took hold.

There was only one thing that truly mattered to her: Leo was alive. He was still sitting on the ground staring in disbelief as the rain pelted Nikolai's lifeless body.

Swallowing down a rush of emotion, she ran over to him, knelt down and threw herself into his arms. "For a second, I thought I had lost you." She rained kisses over his damp face, combed her fingers through his hair to convince herself what she had witnessed was not just another form of mind manipulation.

"I thought so, too," he replied before kissing her softly on the mouth. "I still can't believe he's dead."

Loud cheers behind them captured their attention and Ivana turned to see Elliot and Alexander embracing Sylvester's hulking frame. They took it in turns to pick him up and twirl him around. For the first time in years, her loyal servant's mouth curled up in genuine amusement.

She wanted to hug him, too, for risking his life to save them.

"Can you bloody well believe it," Elliot shouted shaking Sylvester by the shoulders. "I've never been one for gentlemanly conduct." Elliot mimicked Sylvester's words before turning and thrusting his arm forward in an attempt to re-enact the moment the spear pierced Nikolai's chest.

"You certainly took the devil by surprise," Alexander added.

Elliot caught their gaze. He left Alexander hugging Sylvester and raced over to put his hand on Leo's shoulder. "Someone up there must be looking out for you, my friend."

The comment caused a shiver to run through her body. Her heart was still bleeding. The pain of anticipating the loss of her love was still raw.

Leo gave a weary sigh. "I'm damn lucky. But I should have listened to Ivana. I was foolish to think I stood a chance against him."

"I have to say you were remarkable with a sword." Elliot nodded with approval. "I think if it had been a fair fight based purely on skill you would have won."

"And you're not biased in any way." The smile touching Leo's lips went some way to heal Ivana's wounds.

"Not at all." Elliot chuckled. "Indeed, I wonder if Calvino

still tutors at night. I might take a few lessons so you will have someone to parry with once we are home."

The mere mention of Leo going home caused a sudden pang of grief to fill Ivana's chest. She came to her feet, assisted Elliot in helping Leo up as he seemed tired after his mental and physical ordeal.

"You do know I will not be returning to England." Leo's tone was solemn, but Ivana's heart soared. "Not for the foreseeable future. I plan to stay here with Ivana if she has no objection."

Ivana clutched Leo's arm tight to show her approval. They were free to live together in the castle without fearing a devil would come knocking. They could marry; they could sleep in each other's arms every night without repercussions.

Elliot gave a heavy sigh, blinked away the droplets of rain on his lashes. "I suspected you might. If there is anything you need me to do, just ask."

"If you could deliver a letter to Mr. Greaves, he will continue to oversee the running of my estate. But we will discuss it tomorrow." Leo glanced down at his sodden breeches. "We should go inside. I could do with a hot bath and something soothing to drink."

Ivana licked her lips at the thought he might drink from her again. "I believe Julia has already anticipated your needs and has scuttled off to heat the water." In truth, her maid had found the gruesome sight of a headless corpse disturbing. She turned to Elliot. There were many things to discuss; there was no point waiting. "I assume your wives stayed in the village."

Elliot snorted. "We had a battle of our own persuading them it was the most sensible course of action. But from the tone of Leo's note, I sensed the situation was grave."

"You're welcome to take my carriage if you wish to bring them here," Ivana said. "After such a terrifying ordeal, I would not feel happy asking anything more of Sylvester tonight."

Elliot smirked. "If they discovered we had declined an invitation on their behalf, the journey home would be more than uncomfortable." He inclined his head respectfully, yet she still sensed a slight awkwardness which was only to be expected. "Thank you. Alexander will accompany me."

"Do you need to drink first?" she asked. A bolt of desire shot through her as her gaze drifted to Leo's neck.

Elliot shook his head. "No. I suggest we all dine together on our return. I believe there are many things that must be said."

"Dine?" Ivana scrunched up her nose. "On blood? You make it sound as though we are to feast with a king."

Leo draped his arm casually over her shoulder, the sodden material feeling cold against her nape. "You should know, Elliot likes to keep things as civilised as possible. We have a hell of a job getting the red stains out of the table napkins."

Alexander strode over to join them. "Your coachman, Sylvester, deserves a knighthood for his loyalty. By God, who wouldn't want a man like that as a protector?"

Ivana nodded. "He has been my friend and confidante for many years. Indeed, I owe him my life."

"As we all do," Elliot added. He turned to Alexander. "I'm taking the carriage to the village to collect Grace and Evelyn. I assume you want to come."

"Evelyn will be furious to know she has missed it all," he replied with a sigh.

Ivana wondered if they knew the horror that would have unfolded had their wives accompanied them to the castle. "You made the right decision leaving them behind. Had they been here, Nikolai would have used them against you. He would have manipulated their minds, turned them in front of your eyes. It would not have been pleasant to witness."

Alexander's expression grew dark. "I cannot even bear to think of it. But he is dead now and so we must celebrate the victory."

"Good Lord," Ivana gasped suddenly, remembering Nikolai had arrived in a carriage. "I assume Nikolai's carriage has been stabled in the outer courtyard. But where is his coachman? We cannot let him leave to tell the tale of what happened here."

"Sylvester will know," Elliot said. "I will wipe the coachman's memory of this night, make him believe he is to wait for his master in the next town and send him on his way. I doubt Nikolai would have informed anyone of his reason for coming here."

"Nikolai never discussed his private affairs." It occurred to her to mention the cure, but they were all soaked to the skin, all in need of dry clothes and good company, and there was still work to do.

A sudden clap of thunder caused them all to look up to the heavens.

"Do you think God is applauding our efforts?" Ivana asked, wrapping her arms around Leo's waist. "Do you think he is pleased now that he has one less devil to contend with?"

"Most certainly," Elliot replied. "I must also applaud your efforts, Ivana, for caring for my son in my absence. When I return, I would like to discuss the matter with you if I may."

Ivana inclined her head. "Of course. But for the moment, I suggest we go inside and spend a few minutes by the fire. Our lips are blue, and I think it will take more than a vial of blood to restore them to their natural hue."

Leo glanced at the body littering the courtyard. "Once

Elliot has dealt with the coachman, what shall we do with Nikolai?"

Ivana shrugged. When it came to Nikolai, her heart was cold, empty. She could not rouse even a sliver of pity. "We will do what he threatened to do to me once. We will leave him there until the sun rises. Then we will venture outside come nightfall and watch the pile of dust blow away in the wind."

A little over an hour later, they all sat around the long table at the far end of the Great Hall. The fire roared in the hearth, and Ivana feared it would take weeks to warm their bones. As expected, both Grace and Evelyn were ecstatic to be at the castle, and despite learning of Nikolai's fate, the ladies had been spared the true horror of the ordeal.

Ivana sat at the head of the table and watched in wonder as Elliot popped a piece of beef into his mouth. "Do you not retch when you chew it?"

"I did at first." He dabbed his lips with a napkin and raised his goblet of blood in salute. "But now I have mastered the art."

"Does it not taste strange?"

"No. Even though it's cooked, I can still taste the essence of blood."

Ivana could not help but smile. It did feel rather more civilised to sit and watch others eat. She could not participate. Any food at the castle was for the servants' consumption. There had been enough to provide a few small meals, but she did not want to empty the larder completely.

Fear played a part, too. She was scared. She had finally come to terms with the nature of her affliction, accepted who she was now. The sense of hopelessness had eased over the years. To go back, to act as though she was human would only serve to open old wounds.

Of course, things would be different if they found the cure.

The thought caused her heart to race.

Since Nikolai's death, no one had mentioned it. Perhaps they suspected it was a lie used as a form of bribery. Perhaps they were all relieved to be alive and could not think past that. Whatever the reason, she owed it to them to divulge what she knew.

How would they take the news?

How would they cope with the disappointment if they failed to find it?

The need to calm her nerves, to feel a wave of tranquillity wash over, pushed to fore. She wished she had emptied her blood into a goblet as a sip of the burgundy liquid would surely bring instant relief.

Ivana cleared her throat to rouse their attention. "There is a matter of some importance we should discuss." She resisted the urge to jump to her feet in eagerness, to race from room to room emptying drawers and cupboards. "Something that affects all of us."

Elliot placed his cutlery on his plate and coughed into his napkin as he stood. "Forgive me. But before you continue, I would like to speak if I may."

Ivana inclined her head. "Of course," she said, suppressing her impatience.

"I have no secrets from the people around this table," Elliot began, taking his wife's hand as she sat by his side. "Leo and Alexander are my kin, family I would have never come to know had it not been for the terrifying nature of our affliction. Now we are brothers in every sense of the word."

Evelyn picked up her napkin and dabbed at the corner of her eyes.

"God saw fit to send me an angel." Elliot brought Grace's hand to his lips and kissed it tenderly. "To guide me, to show me what it means to love another. I see the same sense of hope in Alexander's eyes when he looks at Evelyn. Now I see it in Leo's eyes, too."

Ivana stared at him, mesmerised by his strength of presence. He appeared so different from the licentious rake she had met in the mausoleum. It eased her guilt to know that through his experiences he had become a better man.

"Ivana." He bowed graciously. "I cannot completely understand your motives for cursing us with such a monstrous affliction. But I am assured you believed your reasons to be just. And so, I extend the hand of friendship. I offer you my thanks, for my brothers and my friends, for the angel at my side and for caring for the sweet boy I am yet to meet."

A pain in Ivana's throat forced her to gulp. She tried to speak, but she struggled to form the words. When her gaze locked with Leo's, her heart felt so full she thought it might burst from her chest. Was this what if felt like to be truly happy?

As Elliot sat down, all heads turned her way. She knew she should stand and say something in response, but feared her legs lacked the strength to support her body.

Sucking in a breath, she gripped the arms of the chair. "Despite the curse I placed upon you, it warms my heart to know ... to know you have flourished, found peace and joy. For many years, this house has been a place of fear. It has been a place where hatred lingered in the shadows. Where despair walked the empty corridors at night. Now it is a place of friendship and love and hope." With the absence of a goblet, she raised her hands in the air. "And so I ask you to dedicate your toast to happiness, whatever form it may take."

The gentlemen raised their goblets. Ivana joined them in their cheers: a heartfelt good riddance to her nightmares and soon the conversation erupted around her. There were but a few hours left until dawn, yet her guests appeared to be comfortable, relaxed.

"You are all welcome to stay here," Ivana said, enjoying the noise and bustle after years of sitting alone in deathly silence.

Evelyn glanced at her husband and smiled. "That would be wonderful if it's not too much trouble."

"Not at all. I shall ask Julia to prepare the rooms." She turned her attention to Elliot. "Tomorrow we shall visit Herr Bruhn and the children. But for the hours remaining, I must bring your attention to the matter I mentioned earlier."

Leo cast her a quizzical glance and leant towards her. "Do you wish to speak of the cure?" he whispered.

She couldn't concentrate with his mouth so close to her ear, and she shivered as she imagined him trailing kisses down the column of her neck. "I do."

Leo sat back and inhaled deeply.

Ivana stood. "As I am sure you are all aware, Nikolai was an expert in mind manipulation. He made me forget many things, memories from the first few days we spent together here. Upon his death, those memories were restored to me." She shrugged and threw her hands in the air. "Do not ask me how such a thing is possible as I do not know. What I can tell you is that Nikolai was a man who wanted everything. He wanted the strength and ability to control the minds of his people. He wanted to walk in the sun and raise offspring to bolster his army. To possess the power to flit between night and day gave Nikolai an advantage over his enemies. Such a feat is only achieved by drinking an elixir that cleanses the blood."

"Cleanses the blood." Alexander straightened as he repeated her words. "Do you mean the cure for our affliction?"

Evelyn gasped as her eyes grew wide with disbelief. "There is a cure for the disease that ails them?"

"I believe so, yes," Ivana replied. "I had a vague recollection of biting Nikolai. Now, I know he suffered from the affliction when he bit me. I know he used me to bite him again once he had taken the elixir."

Elliot cleared his throat. "And you think he came back here to cleanse himself again?"

"I do. The cure is hidden somewhere in this castle. I have never seen it and Nikolai never mentioned where he kept it."

They all fell silent as they scanned the Great Hall, their gazes drifting up to the wooden arches and moving to the stuffed animal heads littering the walls.

"There must be many rooms here," Grace said.

Ivana nodded. "There are forty-three if you count the dungeons."

"You said it is an elixir." Leo touched her arm affectionately as he spoke. "So we are looking for a vial, a bottle or something similar."

Ivana raised her brows and shrugged. "I assume so."

Leo suddenly jumped to his feet. "Well, if there is a cure lying somewhere in this castle, I do not intend to sit around discussing the matter. Where will I find paper and ink?"

"On the desk in the study." Ivana stared at him and pointed to the door at the end of the hall. "It's along the corridor, the second door on the left. Why, what do you intend to do?"

"I'm going to draw a map. I'm going to start at the top and work my way down until I find what we're looking for."

Alexander and Elliot stood too.

"It will be quicker if we all work together," Elliot suggested. "We have a few hours until sunrise and can continue tomorrow evening."

Grace stood up. "Evelyn and I can search the rooms during the daylight hours."

Leo smiled. "Just think, come the morning we might never have to worry about being caught in the sun again."

Collectively they sucked in a deep breath.

Ivana was not prone to fanciful musings, but she closed her eyes and imagined sitting on the grass, eating fruit while the sun warmed her skin. Leo was at her side shielding his eyes from the brilliant rays; their children ran about laughing and giggling whilst at play. Life appeared heavenly.

Dare she hope such an idyllic dream could be possible?

Or like a skilled partner in a game of chess, would Nikolai have anticipated their move.

CHAPTER 18

*L*eo took paper and a pot of ink from the study, and they all made their way to the tower bedchamber.

"It will be quicker if we divide into pairs," Alexander suggested as they gathered beside the bed.

That had been Leo's initial thought. He trusted his brothers to do a thorough job, but if they failed to find the cure, the compulsive part of his nature would force him to scour the rooms again.

"I think we should stay together," Leo said, feeling more confident in his decision. "Ivana's knowledge regarding the history and layout of the castle will be invaluable. None of us would notice if a painting or an item of furniture was missing or out of place. There is a possibility she might remember something important."

Elliot nodded. "I agree. The castle is Ivana's home. It is only fitting she should decide how best to proceed."

Ivana clasped her hands together in prayer and tapped the tips of her fingers to her lips. After a moment's silence, she said, "Leo is right. There is every chance another memory will return as we walk through the corridors. We will stay together. That way we will all be confident nothing has been missed."

Leo placed the paper and ink on the side table. "If we are staying together, there is little point in me drawing a plan." He turned to Ivana. "Is this the only room on this level?"

Ivana nodded. "Yes, but as I spend every night in here, I think I would know if Nikolai had hidden anything in this room."

Leo agreed. He imagined Nikolai would hide it somewhere obscure. In a place where few people had need to venture. "Are there four floors including this one?" Even though he had been a guest at the castle for a few days, he had spent most of his time in Ivana's bedchamber.

Ivana muttered a few words as she counted on her fingers. "Five if you include the dungeon. But it is just a row of single cells. There are no furnishings, no pictures or distinguishing marks on the wall."

"It could be concealed behind a loose block of stone," Alexander offered, "although I imagine it's rather dank down there."

Elliot cleared his throat. "I would expect the bottle or vial to be kept in a vault or a chest. Such a fragile item could not be left open to the elements. Surely Nikolai would not risk it being broken or contaminated."

"I know it is not the same," Evelyn said eagerly. "But my aunt once bought me a small selection of perfumes. The tiny glass bottles were kept in a small padded case. Perhaps the cure is stored in something similar."

"I have never seen anything of that description in any of the rooms," Ivana mused.

Leo turned to face her. He stroked her cheek, fought the urge to claim her mouth. "Where would you hide the cure if you were Nikolai?"

Ivana smiled in response to his affectionate gesture as she considered his question. "Nikolai has not been back to the castle for years. There are certain rooms that are used daily, and I would be surprised if he had stored it in there. The elixir is important to him. So much so, he would have killed us all to prevent us from discovering more about it. If I had the cure, I would hide it in a place no one knows exists."

Leo narrowed his gaze. "Do you mean somewhere like a secret vault or chamber?"

"Many castles and old houses have hidden rooms," Alexander said. "I have seen priest holes behind oak panels, secret corridors behind bookcases, a concealed flight of stairs leading down to God only knows where."

Grace spoke up. "Has there ever been any mention of a secret room? Often you hear tales of such things in the village, stories that have been passed down through generations."

"I have heard mention of previous owners." Ivana nodded. "One of them was thought to have been obsessed with witchcraft. I was warned there may be charred bones buried in the crypt, told I may experience terrifying nightmares. But due to the nature of our affliction, I have never paid it much heed."

Leo pursed his lips. Nikolai said he had inherited the castle from a friend, a man of some wisdom. Someone with knowledge of magic or medicine must have helped him to develop a cure.

"Nikolai said the castle belonged to a great scholar named Talliano. Has anyone ever heard of him?" Leo scanned their blank expressions as they shook their heads. "Nikolai said he came back for the cure and for Talliano's notes. He threatened to burn the place to the ground before he left, including everything else in it."

"Surely his interest in the fellow's notes must have something to do with the cure," Elliot folded his arms as he perched on the end of the bed. "Perhaps Talliano experimented with medicine. Perhaps he used his knowledge to heal."

Evelyn's eyes grew wide. "Herr Bruhn said many people come here for the healing waters. There is a waterfall up in the hills, no more than a mile away. People say it flows from Heaven."

Alexander nodded. "I've heard it mentioned, but thought it was gossip spun by the locals as a way of securing more visitors."

"If Talliano is a man of medicine, then we are looking for a room that has been used as a laboratory," Leo said confidently. If Talliano had invented a cure, it would not have been a simple process. "My guess is that it is below ground level."

Evelyn gripped Alexander's arm. "I know I should remain calm and not get excited, but the thought of a cure warms my heart."

Alexander kissed the top of her head tenderly. "We must expect disappointment, my love. And we must also remember that whatever we find here belongs to Ivana."

Evelyn sighed. "I know."

"It is strange," Ivana mused. "Most people would sell their soul for a chance of immortality. Yet here we all are desperately clinging to the hope that we will one day age and die."

Elliot shot off the bed, the colour draining from his face as his frantic gaze shot to Alexander. He turned to Grace, opened his mouth to speak but froze.

"What do you mean you hope to age?" Grace asked in an innocent tone. "Everyone ages."

Leo suspected that neither of his brothers had told their

wives they were immortal. His heart went out to them as no man wanted to see pain in the eyes of the woman he loved.

Ivana's fearful gaze flitted between the two gentlemen. "Forgive me. I assumed they knew."

Evelyn frowned. "Assumed we knew what? To what do you refer?"

Alexander pushed his hand through his mop of dark hair. He grasped Evelyn's hands and stared soulfully into her eyes. "There is no easy way to say this, and so it is best to say it quickly. One consequence of our affliction is that we are immortal."

Evelyn jerked her head back as her mouth fell open.

"Immortal?" Grace gasped. "But such a thing is not possible."

Elliot took a step towards her, and Grace took a step back. "Alexander speaks the truth."

"You mean you cannot die?" Evelyn's eyes were almost bulging from their sockets. She snatched her hands from his grasp as Grace came to stand at her side.

"We do not age, Evelyn." Alexander gave a heavy sigh. "Therefore, we will not die unless we are caught by the sun, starved of blood, lose our head."

Leo expected to see tears flowing; he had expected to hear sorrowful wails echoing through the chamber, and he held his breath in anticipation.

Evelyn thrust her hands on her hips. "You mean to tell me when I am wrinkled and haggard you will still look like this?" She waved an irate hand down his body and then stamped her foot.

Alexander inclined his head.

"And neither of you thought it was important enough to tell us." She hooked arms with Grace.

"We did not want to hurt you," Elliot said solemnly as he

came to stand at Alexander's shoulder. "Please say something, Grace."

Grace shook her head. "I can understand why you didn't tell us. But I don't know how I can be happy, knowing one day I will be gone, and you will still be young, free to marry again."

"That will never be the case," Elliot replied. "We have made a pact. As you draw your last breath so will we."

Evelyn stared at him and then looked at Alexander. "A pact? Then perhaps Grace and I will make a pact. Perhaps we will ask Ivana to turn us too. Then we will never be apart."

Ivana sucked in a breath. "I'm sorry. But I could not do it. Please do not ask it of me."

"Damn right she won't do it," Alexander roared.

"But why?" Evelyn implored. "Don't you want to live with me forever? Don't you want to love me for all eternity?"

"I will love you for all eternity. There will never be anyone else for me." Alexander closed his eyes and sighed. When he opened them again, Leo could see his pain. "This is not living, Evelyn. Everything about it is unnatural. There is still hope for us. I am convinced we have lived a life together before, and we will do so again. But not like this."

Ivana clutched Leo's arm and put her head on his shoulder. A dark cloud descended. With it came the reality of how difficult it was to live with their terrible affliction.

Elliot held his hand out to Grace and whispered, "Just let me love you."

She stared at it for a moment before running into his arms.

Leo and Ivana watched as both couples embraced, muttered endearments, soothed their souls.

Nothing could break the bond of true love. He believed that now. In his meditative mood, he glanced out through the window; slivers of orange tinged the dark grey sky. Time was both a blessing and a curse. In an hour, the sun would edge up over the horizon, and they would be relegated to the shadows once more. Finding the cure seemed more important than ever, but all he wanted to do was curl up in bed with Ivana and forget the rest of the world existed.

"We must head down to the lower levels before sunrise." Leo straightened as he took Ivana's hand.

"We can still search the Great Hall, the crypt, and the dungeons," Ivana informed them.

"Regardless of what we do or do not discover, know that fate binds us all together." Leo thought it best to be realistic. "Sometimes failure reaps unexpected rewards."

Elliot narrowed his gaze as a smirk played on his lips. "When did you become a man of great sentiment?"

Leo shrugged. "As you know, love has a way of rousing emotion even in the most cold-hearted rakes."

They spent an hour scouring the Great Hall: tapping on wooden panels, peering behind paintings in search of hidden doors. Once Leo was satisfied there were no other places to look, they moved to the crypt.

The underground chamber consisted of a series of aisles divided by limestone pillars, each one flaring up to the vaulted ceiling. The stone's golden hue illuminated what would have ordinarily been a dark room. Leo noticed the arched recess to his left, admired the highly colourful painting of a celestial scene decorating the stonework. As he stepped into the centre of the room, he saw that each wall had a similar recess, all embellished in the same artistic way.

"My, it's so cold down here." Evelyn crossed her arms over her chest and shivered visibly.

Alexander shrugged out of his coat and draped it around her shoulders.

"Mind your head as you walk through." Ivana pointed to where the diagonal rib curved down to meet the pillar. "The ceiling is quite low in places."

"I assume there used to be burial tombs in here." Elliot stamped on the tiled floor with the heel of his boot. "If you look closely, you can see where they would have been."

"I imagine so," Ivana said as she came to stand at his side.

Leo scanned the room. "Perhaps Talliano used this as his laboratory though I wonder what happened to his equipment."

Evelyn walked over to one of the recesses. "The paintings are beautifully done. I suspect whoever was buried down here must have been quite a grand person indeed."

Leo came to examine it. "They all depict various impressions of the gates of Heaven." Indeed, the walls were painted with images of angels holding trumpets. The hues of gold and blue were soothing yet uplifting. "The theme would suggest this was a final resting place. I wonder why they painted it on the wall and not on board or canvas."

"Perhaps they feared someone would steal the paintings." Evelyn ran her hand over the stone wall. "I would have expected them to fade after all this time, but then there is no natural light down here."

The sound of heavy footsteps descending the stairs captured their attention.

Sylvester appeared. "I didn't mean to interrupt, but I thought this might be important." As they all gathered around, he held out his hand and presented them with an elaborate iron key.

Ivana ran her fingertips over the metal. "Where did you find it?"

"It was sitting amongst the pile of dust littering the courtyard."

Alexander turned to Leo and whispered, "I take it the sun has made an appearance."

Leo nodded. "That must be all that's left of Nikolai." Despite witnessing him meeting his demise, Leo felt relieved to find Nikolai didn't know of a mystical potion to turn back time or a spell to make the dead walk again.

"Thank you, Sylvester." Ivana took the key, and their hero trudged back upstairs. "You were right, Leo. It would seem there is a hidden room in the castle."

"We can't go racing through the corridors during daylight," Leo replied. "So we may as well conduct a thorough search of the crypt before we leave."

They all glanced around the empty room.

Elliot cleared his throat. "I doubt that would take more than five minutes." He put his arm around Grace and she cuddled into him.

Leo sighed. "Well, you can tap the floor with your boot, just to ensure there are no loose tiles concealing a trap door. We will all examine the walls."

They all went off in different directions. Leo inspected another painting, his mind engaged with thoughts of Heaven and Hell as he considered the notion that their affliction meant they were all damned.

The constant thud of Elliot's boot rang through the chamber, to the point Leo thought he could hear it echoing beyond the walls. He shook his head. It was impossible. They were twenty feet or so below ground. He stepped back and stared at the painted alcove. It felt as though the vibrant depiction of the golden gates of Heaven, coupled with the angel gesturing to the lock, were there just to mock him.

In one respect, he supposed the cure was the key needed to access the afterlife: their humanity being necessary for them to gain entrance. He stepped closer again, knocked on the stone wall only to hear a hollow sound.

Bloody hell!

As he ran his frantic hands over the surface of the painting, he could feel the seams of a door. "Ivana. Quick, bring me the key."

A sudden flurry of activity behind him made his heart race all the more.

They all rushed to his side, a nervous tension vibrating in the air as eager eyes examined the painting.

"I … I cannot see anything." The tremor in Ivana's voice echoed his own feelings of excitement. Trembling fingers handed him the key. "What is it? Is there a door?"

Elliot leant forward and narrowed his gaze. "Look at the keyhole on the gate. The artist has done a superb job of concealing it."

Leo swallowed deeply before stepping forward.

Time stopped.

Not a single sound could be heard, not even their ragged breathing for they all held their breath in anticipation. The small iron key slipped into the hole in the wall. With two turns and a click, the door shifted just a hair's breadth from the jamb, but Leo felt a soft breeze of air brush over his face.

Ivana gasped. "Is it a room?"

"We will soon see." Leo placed his palms on the flat surface and pushed gently. An icy chill settled over him as he stepped into the small tomb. While the golden limestone blocks in the crypt made the room feel bright, the walls in the tomb were a dull, dreary grey. "It's too dark in here."

"Grace and I will go and ask Sylvester to light some candles," Evelyn said. She gave Alexander his coat before they raced to the stairs.

"Follow me inside." Leo shuffled forward. "But have a care. We do not want to break anything."

They all crept inside; a sense of awe and wonder flooded his chest, and he knew his brothers felt it, too. This tiny chamber could contain the answer to their prayers. As they stood huddled in the centre of the room, they scoured their surroundings.

"The longer I stand here, the clearer the objects in the chamber become," Alexander said, squinting in the darkness.

"I can't believe I have lived here all this time and knew nothing of this secret room." Ivana touched his hand. "Do you think we will find the cure in here?"

Leo sighed. "We can but hope." A strange sense of foreboding settled over him. Perhaps his anxiety stemmed from knowing Nikolai was not a man to be trusted. Perhaps a fear of the unknown caused mild panic to flare.

What would it be like to be human again?

In the years he'd spent coming to terms with the nature of the affliction, he never dared to ask himself the question. To walk in the sun, to eat ham and eggs for breakfast, were but simple pleasures most people took for granted, yet he would have sold his soul to experience them once again.

But things were different now.

Ivana was his life, his love, the greatest gift, the only pleasure. In those terms, his affliction changed nothing. It was neither a hindrance nor a blessing, and so he would not be disappointed if their efforts were in vain.

Evelyn and Grace returned carrying a candlestick in each hand. As soon as they entered the chamber, the golden glow illuminated the table at the far end. Leo took one from Evelyn's hand and placed it on the wooden surface while he inspected the equipment. The others were placed in various positions around the room.

"It looks like some sort of filtering device," Elliot said, touching the glass tube leading into a bulbous bottle. "This piece of muslin could have been used to remove impurities."

Leo shrugged. "Such contraptions mean nothing to me."

"I think these are Talliano's notes," Alexander said. He was sitting behind a desk at the opposite end of the room, flicking through a leather-bound book. "It's all in Latin. His writing is appalling unless he was drunk when he scrawled the words."

"There's a chest on the floor over here." Grace knelt down in front of the small wooden trunk. "It's not locked."

Leo and Elliot came to stand behind her. "Open it."

With hesitant fingers, she raised the lid. "There's nothing inside but a piece of rock."

"Rock?" Leo bent down and peered into the chest. He removed the grey, silvery lump. Its shiny metallic lustre sparkled in the light. "I have no idea what it is."

"In Latin it is known as *haematītes*," Alexander said, coming to stand with them. "Talliano mentions it in his notes. From what I can read, the scholar believed it removed impurities from the blood."

Leo frowned. "Do you suppose we are to ingest a fragment of the stone?" He shook his head. "Surely not."

"There is something under this tray," Grace said, removing the wooden structure that had supported the stone. "There is a box underneath." With steady hands, she removed it and carried it over to the table before placing it down gently.

They all came to stand before the inlaid mahogany box.

No one spoke for a few seconds, but it felt like hours.

"One of us will need to open it," Elliot eventually said with slight apprehension.

Leo turned to Ivana. "Perhaps you should. After all, the contents belong to you."

Ivana grasped his arm. "No. You open it."

Leo sucked in a breath before flicking the tiny brass catch and lifting the lid. Five small brown bottles lay nestled amidst a bed of burgundy silk.

Leo stepped back, his hands were shaking. His heart thumped hard in his chest. "Good Lord. I think we have found the cure."

Excitement thrummed in the air until the whole room vibrated with suppressed hysteria. Leo removed the first bottle, picked out the stopper and sniffed. He could smell nothing. He shook it. But he did not hear the liquid sloshing against the glass. Holding out his hand with his palm facing up, he attempted to pour a drop out for all to see.

But the bottle was empty.

His throat grew tight as he tried to swallow. Leo turned to see their smiles fade, to see fear flash in their eyes. He checked the next bottle, knowing that there were only four left, not knowing what to do should it be empty too.

Replacing the empty bottle back in its cushion, he took the next one, knowing as soon as he held it in his hand it was also empty. Still, he went through the motions, felt his shoulders sag as he tipped it upside down and shook it.

The room was deathly silent.

Leo continued with his ministrations, feeling a little easier when he discovered nothing in the third bottle. To leave only one of them suffering from the affliction would be the worst punishment of all. After checking the last two bottles, it was as he suspected.

He closed the lid gently and turned to face them. In their disappointment, they had stepped back into the middle of the room. Alexander and Elliot held their wives in their arms.

Indeed, the realisation that their husbands were immortal, and there may be no cure, had finally roused painful emotions.

Elliot cleared his throat. "From your grim expression, I suspect it is not good news."

Leo gazed at the sorrowful look on their faces. "I'm afraid we cannot all take the cure."

"All?" Elliot asked. "You mean not all the bottles were empty?"

Leo shook his head, struggled to suppress the wave of sadness consuming him. "No, not all the bottles were empty. There are two left. Only two of us can take the cure."

CHAPTER 19

*T*he sudden sound of whimpering permeated the stunned the silence.

Ivana glanced at the men whose lives had been forever altered by her bitterness and resentment. Their wives looked weak and helpless when enveloped in their strong arms. Many times, while tending to a child plagued with a fever, while trying to persuade Christoph to speak, she had felt justified in her actions. But now she had come to know Evelyn and Grace, to know the love they shared with their husbands, it made her doubt her decision.

Ivana pushed past Leo, desperate to see the evidence for herself. But she knew her eyes and ears had not deceived her. Watching Leo check the bottles, counting in her mind all the times Nikolai had taken the cure, convinced her there was not enough to save them all.

"I thought it might be in a large flask or similar vessel." She ran her hands over the tiny bottles as though the process would make them magically refill. She turned to Leo as he came to stand at her side. "I hoped there would be enough for all of us." Years of suppressed emotion filled her throat, and she gasped a breath. "What can we do, Leo?"

Alexander cleared his throat. "Forgive me, but I need to take Evelyn somewhere to sit down. Is it safe for me to go up into the Great Hall?"

Ivana turned to him, her heart aching when she noticed Evelyn's blotchy face. "In an hour or two. I'm afraid you will have to wait in the crypt until then."

He nodded to the room beyond the secret chamber. "We'll sit out there. It will give you a chance to talk privately."

Elliot looked at Grace, cupped her face and kissed her softly on the lips. "Are you all right?"

She shook her head numerous times in response. "It never mattered to me before, that you were different. But now," she paused and hung her head. "Now I feel as though there is a huge divide separating us. Every day I age only serves to widen the gap, only serves to take me further away from you."

Elliot glanced at them, his rueful look causing guilt to flare. "We will go and sit with Alexander." He took Grace's hand and led her from the room.

Ivana fell into Leo's arms. "Oh, it is all so terrible. It is all my fault."

"Do not be so hard on yourself." He stroked her hair, the motion going some way to soothe her. "We have all moved beyond the need to apportion blame. We all understand you did what you thought was best. Indeed, in a strange way, our lives have been enhanced by our experiences."

She looked up at him and without another word gripped his shirt and claimed his mouth. The kiss was desperate and rough, a way to banish the pain of regret. Even in her despair, she wanted to feel his naked body covering hers. And she would have given anything to join with him in that instant.

Leo stroked her cheek as their lips parted. "We must decide what to do."

"Will we ever be truly happy?" The question fell from her lips without thought. "Will we ever be able to move forward?"

"While my heart aches for my brothers, it soars with joy at the thought of sharing my life with you."

"I love you," she said, a radiant light flowing through her body at the thought.

Leo smiled weakly. "And I love you, which is why I must be honest with you now."

Fear sparked in short, sharp bursts. "You're not going to take the cure, are you? You're going to go back to England with your brothers to live as you did before."

Her mind was a jumbled mess of chaotic thoughts.

He smiled. "If you think I could go and leave you here, then you do not know me at all."

"I'm scared, Leo," she admitted. "You don't know how hard it was for me to say goodbye to you. I don't ever want to feel that way again."

"And you won't." He took her hand, brought it to his lips and kissed it tenderly. "I want to stay here with you. I want us to be married. I want us to live with our affliction so we can give my brothers the chance of living a normal life with their wives."

She stared at him while the gravity of his words penetrated her addled mind. He wanted her to give up all hope of walking in the sun, all hope of ever having a child of her own. A moment was all she needed to reach a decision. In truth, she had never expected such dreams to come to pass. She had never thought to reunite with her one true mate. The thought of living an eternity with Leo was reward in itself.

"Very well," she nodded pushing aside all doubts. "We

will give the cure to Elliot and Alexander. I took their humanity in payment for a debt. From what I have witnessed, they deserve some form of recompense for their plight."

"It is the right thing to do, Ivana."

"I know," she said with a heavy sigh. "Shall we go and tell them?"

Leo closed the lid on the mahogany box and secured the catch. Taking her hand, they walked out into the crypt.

Alexander and Evelyn were sitting on the floor against the wall on the far side of the room. His eyes were closed. Evelyn was curled up against him, her head resting on his chest as he stroked her hair. Elliot stood against a pillar. Grace was nestled between his legs and encompassed in his arms. Upon hearing their approach, both couples came to stand before them.

"It was always going to be unlikely we would find the cure and all live happily in human form again." Elliot's words were logical. But his dull eyes and harrowed expression tore at Ivana's heart. "But despite our disappointment, we are truly happy for you both."

Grace nodded in agreement as she held hands with her husband.

Alexander and Evelyn stepped forward.

"Please, do not mistake our subdued response for bitterness," Alexander said. "We, too, are pleased you have another chance of life."

"We want you to be happy," Evelyn said, hugging Alexander's arm. "We do not want you to hide your true feelings from us."

Other than the first time she had said goodbye to Leo, Ivana had spent the last ten years barely shedding a tear. Now, in the space of a few days, she had become a blubbering wreck.

"You are so kind," she said, failing to stop the tears running down her face. They were tears of happiness, she realised. The cure gave her the power to make amends for all the despicable things she had done.

She nudged Leo as she wanted him to be the one to tell them the news. As always, he interpreted her actions without her having to say a word.

"I won't prolong your misery by spouting flowery words of love and friendship," Leo said. "But know that we are both in agreement regarding how we wish to proceed." He paused. "We have decided neither of us will take the cure."

All four of them appeared bewildered. They blinked and shook their heads, glanced at each other, then glanced back at Leo.

"You do not have to spare our feelings," Elliot said with a hint of compassion. "We understand how difficult it must be for you."

"You mean you want to wait," Evelyn clarified. "I suppose there is no need to rush. Now you know it is here you have time to decide what to do."

Leo brushed his hand through his hair. "No. You mistake me. I do not want to take the cure myself. I want to give the cure to my brothers."

"We want Alexander and Elliot to take the last two bottles," Ivana added.

Elliot covered his mouth with his hand to suppress a gasp as he stumbled back.

Alexander put his hands on his knees and bowed his head while he exhaled deeply.

"Why would you do that when you could live a normal life together?" Grace asked as her eyes grew wide in disbelief. "You could both be free of the affliction."

Leo shrugged. "How could we be happy? Love binds us

all together." He glanced at Ivana. "This is the most logical solution to our problem."

"What Leo is trying to say is that we have each other. Whatever we do, we can do together. The same is not so for either of you. While one walks in the day, the other walks at night. While one eats food for sustenance, the other drinks blood." She did not wish to stress the differences in terms of mortality. "This way, the natural balance will be restored. This way, the wrongs of the past will be put right."

"You should take some time to consider it," Elliot managed to say. "You should not be so hasty in your decision."

Ivana smiled. "We have taken all the time we need. Besides, Christoph needs a father who can take him riding across the meadows, who—" Ivana stopped abruptly. Her emotions always ran high when she spoke of the children. "We have made our decision."

Alexander straightened. "Then I thank you both for being so selfless, for giving me a second chance at life."

Elliot echoed his friend's sentiment, and Ivana was somewhat shocked when both gentlemen embraced her.

"I am not afraid to admit the thought terrifies me," Alexander said with a frown. "What if it doesn't work? What if something should go wrong?"

"Don't say that," Evelyn implored, patting him on the arm. "After everything we've been through, I cannot lose you now."

"Are we supposed to drink the liquid in the bottle?" Elliot asked.

"I have a vague memory of Nikolai drinking the cure, yes." Ivana scoured the recesses of her mind. Some memories were still hazy. "But I do not remember it being in little bottles."

Leo walked over to his brothers, hooked an arm around each of their necks. "Come. We cannot leave this room for at least an hour. Let us go and study Talliano's notes in the hope the answer lies there."

It suddenly occurred to Ivana that Elliot must make another decision before he took the cure.

"I promised Herr Bruhn we would go and see the children." Ivana knew how much the old man looked forward to her visits and hated breaking her promises to him. "With Nikolai's surprise arrival, I will have missed a whole day if I do not go this evening." She turned her attention to Elliot. "You must decide if you wish to see Christoph before you take the cure."

Elliot pursed his lips whilst lost in thoughtful contemplation. He looked at Grace, who nodded but said nothing. "If something should go wrong, I would not want to hurt the boy any more than I have already. At present, he is blissfully ignorant of my existence and so the loss will only be mine to bear."

Grace smiled weakly. "I agree. We should wait to make sure the cure works. In the meantime, there is nothing preventing me from leaving the castle. Evelyn could come with me to visit the children, play with them for an hour and convey your apologies to Herr Bruhn for your absence."

Ivana clasped her hands to her chest. "You would not mind?" After the heavy storm, the old man would be worried. He had too much to fret over without Ivana adding to his woes.

"Not at all. It will give us something to do, something to occupy our minds." Grace turned to her husband. "You will not do anything until I return? Promise me you will wait until I am by your side before you attempt to drink the cure."

Elliot nodded and offered a reassuring smile. "I promise.

We will simply look through the notes while we wait for you to return."

"Speak to Sylvester. He will escort you." It would also give her servant something to do. He had been quiet since the incident in the courtyard and Ivana hadn't had a chance to talk to him privately. Killing a man, even one as cold and heartless as Nikolai, still roused feelings of guilt and shame.

The ladies bid their husbands farewell, climbed the stairs and disappeared from view.

Ivana followed the gentlemen into the secret chamber. After spending an hour watching them decipher Talliano's notes, they seemed to be clearer on what needed to be done.

Alexander ran his finger across the scrawled words, stopping periodically before starting back at the beginning. "It says the potion must be drunk after ingesting infected blood. Talliano found that waiting five minutes proved to cause the least pain."

"Pain?" Elliot shivered visibly. "I suppose it will be a similar feeling to the night we were turned, though, other than a fiery heat flowing through my veins I cannot remember much about it."

Elliot's words roused the memory of the night Nikolai first bit her and made her drink his blood. The body's natural instinct was to fight against the foreign liquid in a bid to cleanse it of its impurities. Small, sharp stabbing pains came first, like driving pins into the skin. It was quickly followed by an intense heat like hot coals burning in the belly.

"Then it will not be pleasant," she said solemnly. "But I suspect it will last no longer than a few hours. Leo and I can assist by compelling you to sleep. It works when the mind is weaker but might not be as effective now you can resist thought manipulation."

Elliot narrowed his gaze, a frown marring his brow. "In

your honest opinion, do you believe it is it safe for us to drink?"

Ivana shrugged. "I assume so. Nikolai would not risk his life on a whim. That much I do know. He came here prepared to take it again. But you must heed Talliano's words, be certain you have interpreted them correctly."

While some Latin phrases seemed familiar at first glance, Ivana had no skill with the language and could not help them.

"As I said, we must drink infected blood," Alexander reiterated.

"Leo can drain some of his blood into a vessel." Ivana did not think they would wish to drink her blood again.

Alexander picked up the leather-bound notebook, scanned the page and shook his head. "No. It says the blood must be the hosts. We are to drink our own blood. The healing properties of the stone, and whatever else is in the bottle, will draw out the toxins. Once the process begins, it will continue working until all the blood in the body has been thoroughly cleansed."

Leo gave a heavy sigh. "It's hard to believe it could work. Then again, had someone told me one bite would cause an aversion to the sun and force me to consume nothing but blood, I would have believed them to be a sure candidate for Bedlam."

They all chuckled, but anxiety and apprehension still hung in the air.

"I shall read through the notes once more." Alexander took the book and sat down behind the desk. "When our wives return, I suggest we follow Talliano's instructions and begin the process."

Elliot brushed his hand through his hair and sighed. "In a matter of hours, we may be free to walk in the sun."

Ivana noted the glimmer of sadness in Leo's eyes. Despite

it being his decision for his brothers to take the cure, her heart still ached for him. In a matter of hours, he would be different from his friends. He truly would be alone and abandoned to the night.

CHAPTER 20

"*I* pray everything will work out well," Grace said, touching Evelyn's arm as they hovered at the top of the stairs leading down to the crypt.

Despite spending a pleasant couple of hours with Herr Bruhn and the children, Evelyn's shoulders sagged from the weight of the heavy burden. "I cannot imagine a life without Alexander, and so I must have faith that we were all sent here for a reason. Whatever happens in this castle was always destined to be."

Grace covered her heart with her hand and sighed wearily. "I wish I could share your optimism."

"I may look calm and composed, yet inside my heart is breaking. In truth, I do not want Alexander to take the cure. But then I do not want him to watch me grow old and frail, either. I couldn't bear to see pity in his eyes when I am used to his heated gaze and looks of desperate longing." Evelyn shook her head to eradicate all sorrowful thoughts. Being subdued and downcast would only cause Alexander to worry. "But we must be brave for our husbands. We must let them believe we are confident in their success."

Grace grasped her hand and held it tight. "We will help each other through the next few difficult hours. If you see me looking sad and forlorn, I give you permission to pinch me."

Evelyn smiled. Although they had been friends before the long journey to Bavaria, the three weeks spent confined to the carriage had brought them closer. "It is comforting to know we have each other."

Graced nodded but then her faint smile faded. "I do worry about Ivana. She looked terribly distraught earlier. By rights, the cure belongs to her. It was more than generous of her to offer it to our husbands."

The gesture had helped to ease their husbands' bitterness towards the woman who had changed their lives. Ivana's love for Leo shone like a bright beacon, which had eased their fears for their friend, too.

"Then we will offer her the hand of friendship. We will let her know that we forgive her for everything that has happened before this day." Evelyn knew it was the right thing to do. "Leo loves her, that much is obvious, yet I am still a little confused by it all. We will embrace them as a couple, as our kin."

"You have a kind heart, Evelyn."

Evelyn forced a smile. "Let us hope God sees fit to reward us both for our generous spirits."

They descended the steps to the crypt with a renewed sense of confidence and determination.

"There you are." Elliot came towards them. He took Grace's hand. "We have decided to remain down here when we take the cure. We have no notion how long the recovery period will last and cannot risk being in a room where the sun's harmful rays can penetrate."

Evelyn forced a smile. She stared at Grace, who soon followed her lead. "That sounds like a logical idea." Evelyn glanced at the tiled floor. "But I cannot imagine it will be comfortable."

"That is why we were waiting for your return. We need you to help Sylvester move items from one of the chambers, as we are all bound to the shadows until nightfall."

Evelyn felt the hairs on her nape tingle and knew Alexander approached.

"You're back." He stood behind her, kissed the top of her head affectionately.

Be brave. Don't let him see your fears.

She turned to face him, sucked in a breath at the magnificent sight of his handsome countenance. In her mind, she imagined hugging him, standing on the tips of her toes to feel his soft lips on hers. But she smiled and said, "Did you miss me?"

He took her hand and brought it to his lips. "Always."

Evelyn stared longingly into the steel-blue eyes that had held her captive from the first moment she'd met him. "I love you," she mouthed silently.

The corners of his mouth curved up into a sinful grin.

"We will need pillows and blankets." Elliot's words invaded the tender moment. "Perhaps water and a cloth to wipe the brow."

"We'll go and find Sylvester," Grace said.

Evelyn could hear apprehension in her friend's voice and so glared at her when she swung back around. "Is there anything else we can get you, my lord," she asked in a mocking tone. "Some foot rub perhaps, or a newspaper."

Elliot raised a quizzical brow. "I'm pleased you're still able to tease me despite the gravity of our situation."

Evelyn raised her chin. "I am tired of all these morbid thoughts. All will be well. I am certain of it." She gave a contented sigh in the hope he could not see through her facade. "Now we shall go in search of your provisions."

Sylvester led them to a chamber on the first floor. They collected pillows and as many blankets as they could carry. Ivana had asked them to bring a mattress. Evelyn examined the bedding piled on top of the wooden frame. She doubted Ivana would want them to use the down one and so she folded it back and removed the cheaper flock from underneath. They would need at least five to make lying on the cold floor of the crypt seem appealing.

It was only as the blankets were folded and laid flat on top of the mattress in the crypt that Evelyn realised there was only one bed. The thought of trudging back upstairs made her groan, albeit inwardly.

"That should be suitable," Ivana said, placing her palms on top of the soft padding. "At least it is better than the cold tiles."

Alexander gave a hapless shrug. "Comfort is the least of my concerns."

"Give us a moment and we will go and search for more bedding." Evelyn put her hands on her hips to catch her breath. "Shall we bring the same quantities again?"

"It won't be necessary." Alexander cleared his throat as he struggled to look her in the eye, a sure sign she would not like whatever he had to say. "While you've been busy upstairs, we have decided it would be wise if only one of us took the cure. There is no point both of us suffering unnecessarily. Should there be no problems, then the other will take it."

Evelyn's heart skipped a beat, and she knew then that Alexander would be taking the cure first. "And you did not think to consult your wives when you made this decision?"

Anger, mingled with a sudden sense of panic, infused her tone.

Alexander glanced at the floor. When he looked up, her heart ached at the fear she saw flashing in his eyes. There was a long agonising moment of silence. "Elliot has a son to think of, whereas I do not. It is only right I take the cure first."

"Don't you think I know that?" She did not want to see him suffer. Alexander was her love, her life, her everything. Without another word, she flew into his arms. "Know that I will lie by your side, that I will hold your hand while I wait for you to return to me."

He wrapped his strong arms tightly around her. "I will come back to you." The words were softer than a whisper but had the strength to soothe her tortured soul.

"Then let us get it over with. I cannot bear to stand here waiting, worrying."

He took her face in his hands and kissed her deeply. "Come. It is time."

They stepped apart, stared into each other's eyes for a time. Leo went into the secret chamber and returned with the mahogany box. They all took turns to hug Alexander as though it was the last time they would see him alive. Elliot muttered something about friendship and honour, told him he should not worry about his wife as he would always care for her.

The next few minutes passed quickly.

Alexander forced his fangs from their sheath, bit into a vein at his wrist and sucked a mouthful of blood. They counted five minutes. The muttered whispers were incoherent. With Evelyn's mind distracted by pessimistic thoughts, she lost count many times and, in the end, left it to Leo to decide when her husband should drink the contents of the little brown bottle.

Leo pulled the stopper from the bottle and handed it to Alexander. "I wish you luck, my friend."

Alexander stared at it for a moment. Locking gazes with Evelyn, his hand curled around her arm, and he pulled her closer. The kiss was chaste yet infused with a wealth of feeling.

"I love you," he whispered. "Should anything happen, know that I will find you again."

He did not wait for a response, but drank the liquid quickly, wincing and shaking visibly as though it tasted stale, putrid. They all stared at him with open mouths. The silence was almost deafening as they waited for a reaction: a cry, a groan, anything.

A minute passed.

Nothing.

Alexander closed his eyes as his breathing slowed until it was barely audible. Evelyn tried not to panic; she tried to remain calm. He would come back to her. He had to come back to her. Then without any warning his body twisted, contorted. She could see from his pursed lips that he was suppressing the pain.

"S-something is happening," Alexander stammered. He swallowed multiple times, clutched his throat as he shuddered violently.

"Help me to lie him down," Elliot said, tugging Leo's arm.

Evelyn stood riveted to the spot. Grace put an arm around her shoulder, but it brought no comfort. Not today. Why had she insisted on coming with him to Bavaria? Why had she not begged and pleaded with him to stay with her at Stony Cross? Damn Leo. Damn everyone who sought to rob her of the only thing that mattered.

They laid him down on top of the mattress she had

dragged off the bed. In the garden of Stony Cross, they had stood beside their favourite bench; she had told him how much she loved him, that she was not afraid anymore. Now, just mere months later, she had never been more terrified in her life.

"Loosen his cravat." Elliot barked orders at Leo, the panic in his voice clearly evident. "We should have removed his coat, left him in just a shirt."

Both gentlemen quickly set to the task. One of them held Alexander's writhing body while the other stripped off his clothes, leaving him in just a shirt and breeches.

Alexander's piercing cry shot through the crypt, the painful sound rebounding off the ceiling and hitting her like a shower of knives.

"He feels so damn hot," Elliot complained as he touched Alexander's brow.

Ivana hurried forward with the bowl and the linen cloth. The sound of trickling water was only just audible amongst Alexander's cries and groans. Smoothing the damp cloth over his brow proved to be too difficult a task. With arms flailing wildly, he knocked Ivana back.

"I think we should compel him to sleep," Ivana said as his face turned claret red. "I think we should do it now."

"Very well." Elliot sucked in a ragged breath. "Put your hands on him and will him to sleep."

"Just help him, please." Evelyn's plea was barely louder than a whisper.

Ivana, Elliot, and Leo surrounded Alexander. They knelt beside him, one hand touching his chest, their eyes all closed as they muttered their silent prayers.

Evelyn watched with bated breath, willing them to succeed.

Another minute passed before Alexander's breathing

slowed to a more regular pace. All cries of anguish ceased. The room felt suddenly calm and still like the air after a heavy storm.

Thank heavens. Evelyn sagged with relief. "Sweet dreams, my love."

Hours passed.

Only his faint mumbles, the changing hue of his complexion from alabaster to claret and the odd trickle from his brow alerted them to the fact he was still of this world.

Evelyn lay by his side, despite Elliot's plea for her to rest, to quench her thirst and take sustenance. Nothing else could soothe her now. She closed her eyes, lingered in the place just before sleep, the magical place where one created their own versions of dreams.

"Eve … Eve."

She opened her eyes with a start, sat up and scoured his face. Hope faded when she realised he was still locked in a deep form of stasis. Then his mouth twitched, the top lip rising up over his gum. The white points of his fangs appeared from their fleshy sheath, extending until they touched his bottom lip.

She glanced back over her shoulder to where Leo and Elliot sat on the floor. "Look at this," she said quietly for fear of disturbing Alexander.

They jumped to their feet and rushed over to her side.

"What is it?" they said in unison.

"It's his fangs." Evelyn raised his upper lip fully. As soon as her finger brushed against the odd-shaped tooth, it fell from the gum into her hand. With a gasp, she stared at the shiny white weapon lying in her palm. "What does it mean?"

Was he dying? Was he cured?

"I don't know." Elliot touched the other one, and it came away, too. "Perhaps it is part of the healing process."

Leo sighed. "Do you think we should attempt to wake him?"

A frown marred Elliot's brow. "Let's wait a little longer."

Evelyn curled her fingers around Alexander's fang. It was part of him. The memory of the night she first saw them flashed into her mind, the memory of the first time she had not been afraid. He had led her down to the river, joined with her, loved her. She clenched her hand tight, the treasure inside worth more to her than the rarest diamond.

Grace returned carrying a plate with sliced apple and cheese. "Is he awake?" she asked with excitement.

Evelyn shook her head.

"Here, I brought you this." Grace offered her the plate. "You need to eat, Evelyn. You must stay strong."

Evelyn nodded and put the plate on the floor at her side. "Where is Ivana?"

Grace's lips thinned. "She's sitting in the Great Hall. Watching him like this, seeing the pain, the guilt is too much for her."

"You should stay with her, offer comfort. I'll call you if there is any change."

Grace glanced at Elliot, unable to hide her solemn expression. "We'll call you," he reiterated.

As soon as Grace left them, Alexander began mumbling again. "Eve ... come to me ... save me."

"I am here, Alexander." She put her head on his chest, could hear his heart beating. "I will always be here."

He muttered something incoherent, but it sounded like 'Mrs. Shaw'.

"Mrs. Shaw?" Leo scrunched his nose. "He must be dreaming about Stony Cross."

"She is like a mother to him. She was the only person he had to turn to, the only person to keep him company during those first lonely years." Just saying the words brought a tear to her eye.

Elliot touched Alexander's brow with the back of his hand, raised his lids and peered into his eyes. "I think we should try to wake him."

"I shall call Ivana," Leo said.

"No. Leave her be. If we cannot manage on our own, then we will call her."

Evelyn sat up. "Can I stay?"

Elliot nodded. "Of course."

She watched them place a hand on his chest, decided she would do the same although she knew it would not make any difference. They began their strange mutterings, and so she made her own silent plea.

Wake up, my love. Come home to me. Wake up.

She did not stop until she felt him suck in a deep breath.

"I think he is waking." Elliot lifted Alexander's lids, and they could see his eyes shifting left and right. "Alexander? Can you hear me?"

Evelyn's heart was beating so rapidly she could feel it thumping in her neck.

Her husband mumbled and moaned for a few more minutes but eventually opened his eyes fully. He scanned his surroundings, put his hand to his temple and winced.

"I have ... have the worst throbbing pain," he complained, yet they were the most beautiful words she had ever heard. His eyes fluttered and closed numerous times. "I need to drink," he suddenly gasped.

Fear gripped her, and she could tell by his brothers' expressions that they believed the cure had failed to rid him of his addiction to blood.

"Quick," Alexander gasped, suddenly shooting up to a sitting position. "I need ... I need water."

"Water?" The word rang through the chamber, filling her heart with hope.

Elliot gestured to the opposite side of the room. "There is a pitcher of clean water over there, hurry."

Leo raced to get the pitcher and the pewter mug. When he returned, Alexander snatched the jug from his grasp and drank it down in seconds.

"Good God," Alexander panted before wiping his mouth with the back of his hand. "I … I have never been so thirsty in my entire life."

Without another word, he shot to his feet, swayed from side to side as he tried to find his balance. "Eve."

She jumped up and hugged him tight. "I am here, Alexander. I am here."

"Did … did it work," he muttered. "Am I cured? I can hardly remember a thing about it."

Evelyn stepped back, and they all gaped at him. "You look the same," she said, "although your fangs fell out." She opened her clenched fist. "See."

"Good heavens." He touched his gums with the tip of his finger, then picked up the tooth and examined it closely. "Remarkable."

Leo sighed. "The true test will be when you step outside, my friend."

Alexander looked to the stairs apprehensively. "Is it still daylight?"

"I believe so," Elliot replied.

He held out his hand to her. "Then there is no time like the present."

Evelyn climbed the stairs with her husband. They stood before the large arched door while Elliot and Leo rushed to find Grace and Ivana.

"Are you sure you want to do this?" Evelyn said as she

gripped his hand, knowing their life together hinged on something as simple as stepping beyond the thick piece of oak. "I'm frightened something might have gone wrong."

A loud rumbling noise erupted in his stomach. "My God, I'm starving. Surely that is a sign all is well."

She stared up at him. His striking blue eyes were just as captivating as the first time she'd seen them. The dimple in his chin that conveyed a playful charm still held her spellbound. It was as though the events of the last few hours had never occurred. He looked the same, had the same intoxicating scent.

"Do you feel any different?" she asked as she examined his features.

He shrugged. "I'm a little weak, and hungry, but not for blood." He winced and made a clicking sound with his tongue. "There's a strange metallic taste in my mouth and my head feels heavy, as though I'd downed a whole bottle of brandy last night and am suffering from the aftereffects."

"I suppose it is like recovering from an illness. You should expect to feel this way for a day or two. Once you've eaten, you might feel better and more water will help to ease the pain in your head." She was gabbling, stalling.

Alexander glanced at the oak door. "We cannot delay the inevitable," he said, turning back to caress her cheek. "Open the door, Eve."

With trembling fingers she grasped the iron ring, turned the handle and pulled the door slowly towards her. Thin slivers of light penetrated the darkness, the rays touching his breeches, his shirt.

Alexander instinctively stepped back.

Evelyn froze, unable to open the door fully.

"Just give me a moment," he said, daring to touch the white light with the tips of his fingers.

With a little more confidence, he let the sun's stream envelope his whole hand as Evelyn watched in wonder. Alexander stared at it for a moment, twisting his hand this way and that, examining it, scrutinising.

She heard their friends approaching, heard their gasps as they witnessed what in essence was a miracle.

"Can you feel any pain at all?" Elliot asked incredulously from the gloomy depths of the hallway. "I daren't take a step closer."

"No. I feel nothing." Alexander nodded to the door. "I'm ready to walk outside."

Feeling much more confident, Evelyn opened it fully. She stepped over the threshold out into the courtyard. She had expected to see some remnants of the man who had tried to kill them, but she saw nothing other than a faint dusting of ash covering the cobblestones.

Holding her hands out in front of her, she said, "Come, my love."

Sucking in a breath, Alexander stepped forward. He squinted, covered his eyes with his arm. Years spent hiding in the darkness had taken its toll. Evelyn waited to hear a cry, the sizzling of burning skin, but he lowered his arm slowly to expose himself to the harmful rays.

The fear in his eyes quickly changed to excitement, elation.

He raced forward, picked her up and swung her round and round. "Sweet Lord above, I cannot believe it." His cheers of joy could surely be heard down in the village.

"You're making me dizzy," she laughed, gripping him tight.

He lowered her to the ground, his hungry gaze drifting over her face. "It is so good to see the way the sunlight reflects off your hair, to see its warmth illuminate your skin. Are you pleased I am human again?"

Evelyn cupped his cheek. "I just want you to be happy. I just want to love you." She was aware that their celebrations may cause sadness and regret for Leo and Ivana. "Let us go back inside. Tomorrow, we can spend the day frolicking in the sunshine. But for now, we must think of your brothers."

His lips thinned, and he nodded. "As always, you are right. But just do one thing for me before we go inside, before the sun sets on this glorious day."

"You know you only need ask me and I would do anything for you."

"Kiss me, Eve. Let me feel your warm lips, let the sun beat down on us as we celebrate our love."

A smile touched her lips. She stood on the tips of her toes, brushed his mouth gently, softly. With a groan, Alexander crushed her to his chest, and they were soon lost to the blinding light of their passion.

CHAPTER 21

*E*lliot heard Alexander's jubilant cheers. It gave him hope, a feeling he had not dared let enter his thoughts until now.

Grace raced to the door eager to witness the miracle. "All is well," she called back over her shoulder, her brilliant smile illuminating her eyes as she hugged the jamb. "He is cured."

"I understand it must be difficult for you." He turned to Leo and Ivana, who were his companions in the gloomy shadows. "You could have been human again too."

Leo shook his head. "I would have it no other way. Of course, if it were possible we would drink the cure without hesitation. But I am elated to hear my brother's cries of joy when I know he has suffered for so long."

Elliot put a hand on his friend's shoulder. "As have we all."

Ivana cuddled into Leo's chest as he wrapped his arm around her. "I wish there had been enough for all of us," she said with a sigh. "I wish we could all find a way out of this nightmare. But I, too, take comfort knowing one of us is at peace."

When Alexander and Evelyn came back through the door, happiness radiated from them bold and bright. Knowing that his brothers could not step forward, Alexander came over to them.

"I cannot thank you enough." He hugged Leo, kissed him on the cheek ten times or more before bringing Ivana's hand to his lips and offering a respectful bow.

Amidst their chuckles and expressions of love and gratitude, Elliot glanced at Grace. He knew her well enough to know her weak smile masked a sudden pensive mood. Taking a deep breath, she put her palm to her stomach, nibbled on her bottom lip and observed the merriment like a spectator, not a participant.

"I do not wish to wait any longer," Elliot suddenly blurted. One way or another, he would ease his wife's suffering. When her eyes grew wide, he added, "I am more confident after witnessing Alexander's success."

He held out his hand, used his ability for mind manipulation to ease Grace's troubled thoughts for what would hopefully be the last time.

"You're sure this is what you want to do?" Grace said as her small hand settled into his. "We will still take Christoph home if you've changed your mind."

To be able to walk in the sun with his wife and child, to give Grace the gift of a child of her own, and another one hundred reasons he did not have the time to give thought to, convinced him taking the cure was necessary.

He caressed his wife's cheek, tried to stop his fingers from trembling when he recalled Alexander's terrifying cries as the cure destroyed the poison in his blood. "Come the morning I will walk with you in the sun. When we return home, we will promenade in the park. Eat ices to cool our lips. But during the healing process, I ask that you remain in the Great Hall. I ask you to stay up here with Evelyn until Leo sends for you."

Her bottom lip quivered. "You don't want me to stay with you?"

"I don't want you to be frightened."

Grace shook her head vigorously. "I won't let you go through this alone."

Elliot smiled weakly. "I can feel you with me." He touched his fingers to his heart. "You will always be in here."

"What if I were the one lying on the cold floor of a crypt, writhing in agony?" Grace said abruptly. "Would you sit in the Great Hall warming yourself by the fire?"

Elliot gripped her hand. "Wolves could not tear me away from you," he whispered.

Grace gave a curt nod in recognition, pressed her palm against his and wrapped her fingers around tightly. "Then we understand one another."

They all went down into the chamber, followed the same procedure as before. This time, Ivana had no choice but to stay. Now only two of them had the ability to compel Elliot to sleep.

It felt strange biting into his skin. He had expected the sharp points of his fangs to meet some resistance, like human teeth biting into a tough piece of beef, but they sank into the flesh with ease.

Elliot drank a mouthful of his own tainted blood and swallowed it quickly. He waited the required five minutes before downing the contents of the small brown bottle. The liquid raced down his throat, the sudden sharp pang in his stomach making him jerk.

"What's happening?" Grace said, her frantic gaze darting over him.

"I can feel it trickling through my veins." Elliot closed his eyes briefly as the cure spread through his body. His blood bubbled and boiled in response. "I should lie down."

He did not want them to have to wrestle him to the floor. Shrugging out of his coat and waistcoat, he tugged the shirt from his breeches, fanned the material to cool the burning skin on his chest.

"Shall we compel you to sleep now rather than wait?" Leo asked.

"No. I ... I do not want to do anything that might slow down the healing process." He shuffled on the mattress in a bid to find a more comfortable position. "Just wait a little while longer."

As soon as the cure reached the tips of his toes, he felt an instant change. The fire heating his body suddenly turned cold. Every muscle grew hard and solid. He felt like a piece of scorching metal pulled fresh from the furnace and then dunked into a vat of ice-cold water. He could almost hear the sizzling as his temperature plummeted.

Perhaps his experience would be different from Alexander's: less painful, less intense. It was a foolish thought. Within seconds, his body began to burn again. The first few stabbing pains were bearable but soon attacked him until he felt as though he was being beaten and moulded with a black-smith's hammer.

He could hear his own cries echoing through the chamber, could feel his friends' hands on his chest, their muttered words wishing him to sleep.

"It's taking too long," Leo barked. "Grace, Alexander, kneel beside us. I know you do not have the ability to enter his thoughts, but your strength and prayers may help."

Lost in a swirling black mist, Elliot knew the moment Grace placed her hand on his chest. For some unknown reason, it had the power to soothe him, helped him to fight against the poison in his blood. After what seemed like hours, but could have been minutes, he could feel himself being slowly sucked down into the peaceful realms of sleep. Despite his dazed and confused state, he knew there was only one thing left to say.

"I love you, Grace," he whispered, not knowing if she could hear him as he drifted away.

For a long time, his world felt black: an empty void where he lingered waiting to discover his fate. The first few fragments of dreams were memories of the past: images representing all the licentious things he had done to numb the pain. He suddenly felt guilt and shame, yet at the time he had felt none of those things. Then his world became clearer. Grace entered his field of vision. Like a brilliant star in the night sky, she dazzled him with her magnificence. Where he had once felt cold and alone, he now felt the joy of love and companionship.

"I will never love another, only you." Grace's voice touched him, shook him awake. "I will never stop thinking of you."

He opened his eyes to find her sitting at his side, hugging her knees to her chest as she rocked back and forth. Scanning the chamber, he realised they were alone. His lids felt heavy, and he could not stop them from closing again.

Time passed.

Booted footsteps echoed through the chamber. "Grace. Please, you should come upstairs and rest." He recognised Leo's voice. "There is nothing more you can do here."

"I'll not leave him."

Leo sighed. "But it has been three days. You cannot continue like this."

Three days!

Panic flared. Grace would think the worst. He had to force his eyes open, make her see he still lived and breathed.

"G-grace," he stuttered, his stiff jaw making it difficult to speak. "Don't … don't go."

He heard their shocked gasps, followed by Leo yelling Ivana to come.

Suddenly the sound of excited voices filled the room. Leo and Ivana knelt by his side, whispered the words to wake him fully from his sleep.

It took no effort to force his eyes open for the second time.

"Tell me you're well." Leo patted his chest as he lay on the mattress. "Tell me that the nightmare we've lived these last few days is finally over."

"I am well," he said weakly. He tried to determine how he truly felt. His mouth was tight and dry as though he had been lying face down on the sand. The painful, hollow feeling in his stomach he recognised to be extreme hunger. With some effort, he managed to sit up. "I am certain the cure was effective," he added, confident in the knowledge he felt human again.

Grace threw her arms around him. "I thought I had lost you."

One thing had not changed. All he wanted to do was cover her body with his own and bury himself deep inside the only place he had ever felt truly happy. He kissed her tenderly on the lips, on her cheek, her temple. "I told you, wolves couldn't tear me away from you." He ran the tip of his tongue over his upper gums. They felt sore, swollen, yet normal. "What happened to my teeth?"

Leo handed him a pitcher. "We don't know. We were desperate for a sign to know all was well and when we inspected your mouth, your fangs had disappeared. I thought you might have swallowed them."

"Good Lord, I hope not." He nodded to the pitcher. "I assume it is safe to drink." Thirst prevented him from waiting for a response. The water slid easily down his throat, the taste cool and refreshing. He did not retch or splutter. "Did I hear you correctly? Have I been down here for three days?"

A look of grief flashed in Leo's eyes. "I'd almost given up any hope of you ever waking. We have tried numerous times to rouse you from sleep but to no avail."

Grace hugged him. "I would never have given up."

Elliot stroked her hair as he held her close, noted the absence of his other brother. "Is Alexander well?"

Grace looked up into his eyes. "He slept for hours the first night. But he is fully recovered. He is with Evelyn and the children. We didn't know what to do. I told Ivana to speak to Herr Bruhn, to tell him I wanted to take Christoph home."

The mention of the son he had never met caused a mixture of emotions: regret, sorrow, love, hope.

Ivana stepped forward. "I have spoken to Herr Bruhn. He will be sad to see the children leave," she said solemnly. "But Frau Bruhn is a little better, and he must spend his time caring for her. He is pleased the children will have a family and a home, that their prospects for the future are bright, full of promise. He is aware that life is precarious. That the children must have security. Indeed, Frau Bruhn's illness has only made him worry for their future."

Grace smiled. "We have promised that they will write to the Bruhns, keep them informed of their progress."

Elliot narrowed his gaze, wondering if the cure had affected his hearing. "You said the children. You speak as though they are all coming to England."

Ivana inclined her head. "They are, with your permission, of course."

"Oh, the boys were so distraught to hear of Christoph leaving." Grace spoke so quickly he had trouble keeping up. "I couldn't leave them behind. Oh, say we will take them all, Elliot."

"All?" He swallowed deeply. "How many children are there?"

"Five," Grace blurted. "But both girls are going to live with Evelyn and Alexander."

Good heavens. He had only been asleep for a few days. Now between them, they were responsible for five children. "Do they all want to come with us?"

"They are sad to leave the Bruhns," Grace explained, "but excited at the same time. Leo has given Alexander his carriage so we may all go home together. Oh, I have prayed you would wake up. I could not have left here without you."

Elliot's head still felt heavy, his thoughts a little jumbled and chaotic. What if the human sensations he was experiencing were simply a concoction of an eager imagination? How could he be a father to children if still suffering from the affliction?

"Would you mind helping me up?" he said to Leo, who still hovered at his side. "What time is it?"

Leo assisted Grace in bringing Elliot to his feet. "It is almost nine. Nine in the evening," he replied. "You'll have to wait until the morning before you will truly know if the cure has worked."

"Damn." Elliot exhaled. He was desperate to step out into the sun after four long years hiding in the darkness.

"What's wrong?" There was a glint of fear in Grace's eyes. "The cure has worked. I know it has."

"I am sure it has." The rumbling in his stomach was

surely a sign of success. He turned to Grace. "Come. Let us go up to the Great Hall. I need to eat and would like to spend a little time alone with you. I assume Ivana has allocated a bedchamber."

The glint of desire in his wife's eyes caused his body to flame. Even in his weakened state, he would have no problem attending to their needs.

Ivana cleared her throat. "The children are here, in the castle. It is important they become acquainted with you all before making the final decision to leave. If you feel able, you should meet them. Evelyn is putting them all to bed, but there is still time if you want to see your son."

Grace touched his arm. "Go with Ivana. Let her tell you about Christoph. I shall speak to Julia about supper and wait for you in our chamber."

Elliot closed his eyes briefly and inhaled. How did one atone for abandoning a child? What would he say to the boy? How would he feel?

Grace touched his cheek. "Don't be afraid. The nightmare has passed. You are free to indulge your dreams. You are free to be the man you were always destined to be."

CHAPTER 22

*I*vana led Elliot upstairs to the children's chamber. They stopped outside the door, and she could hear Evelyn's excited voice regaling the folk tales they loved so much.

As her fingers curled around the handle, Elliot put his hand on her arm.

"Before we enter, I would like to know the story of the boy's mother." The nervous edge to his tone was unmistakable. "Who was she? I am ashamed to say I can't remember. What happened to her?"

Ivana nodded, gestured to a place a little further along the dim corridor, and he followed her. "Christoph's mother is the lady you took to the mausoleum."

Elliot's eyes widened, and he covered his mouth with his hand.

"It was not the first time she had been unfaithful to her husband, but he knew the child could not be his and so abandoned her. She came here with a babe in her arms, looking for you. But I knew you would never return, not after what I had done to you."

"Did she tell you the child was mine?"

Ivana nodded. "She did. As soon as he grew, it was apparent she spoke the truth."

"Where is she now?"

"She is dead." Ivana swallowed down the lump in her throat. "Herr Gebert gave her employment at the tavern, in return for food and lodgings. I think she thought to wait for you in the hope you would come back, in the hope you would make a financial contribution to ease her burden."

Elliot turned away, paced back and forth before stopping abruptly. "Was it a fever, an illness that claimed her?"

"No." This was perhaps the part of the tale Ivana struggled to comprehend. "She met another gentleman, not a nobleman like yourself, but a merchant travelling through here. She pleaded with Frau Bruhn to take your child." The Bruhns were the kindest people Ivana knew and would never have refused the chance to give a child a secure home. "She went off with the merchant. They had a carriage accident a few miles from here. Some say the coachman was drunk on ale. That his slow reactions caused the conveyance to come off the road and slip down the muddy bank."

Elliot drew his palm down his face and exhaled loudly. "If Leo had not come back here, I would never have known about the boy."

Ivana wondered if he struggled to use the word *son*. Perhaps he would feel differently when he saw how sweet and good-natured his child was.

"There is something else you should know. Christoph barely speaks. For his age his oral skills are poor. There seems to be no reason for it. I have tried to encourage him over the last few months, yet have achieved only minimal results."

Elliot cleared his throat. "Is he ill? Has he suffered some sort of trauma?"

"What, other than never knowing his father and losing his mother at such a young age?" Ivana could not hide the contempt in her tone, but she no longer had need to apportion blame. "Forgive me. The children mean the world to me."

"After what you have experienced, after all you have done, I cannot condemn you for your opinion. But I seek to make amends for my mistakes. Know that I will not fail him again."

Ivana's heart soared at his words. She felt the truth in them, and that was all that mattered. "I do believe you will be an exceptional father, as exceptional as you are a husband."

Elliot inclined his head. "That is great praise indeed from a woman who despised me to the core of my being."

"We cannot go back and change the past. Both of us have done things we are not proud of, and so I say we draw a line in the sand, agree to move forward in the knowledge we are both better people."

"They are wise words, indeed." He took her hand and brought it to his lips. "Thank you, for taking care of my son. Thank you for loving my brother in the way he deserves."

A sudden well of emotion rushed to the fore. She dabbed at the corner of her eye for fear the tears would fall. "Come," she said, walking back towards the door. "It is time to meet your son."

They entered the room to find Alexander lying in the middle of the bed. The children sat around him staring at Evelyn seated in the chair eagerly reciting her story. They all looked so happy, so carefree, and Ivana's heart swelled.

Alexander shot up as soon as his gaze met Elliot's. "You're awake." He clambered from the bed, rushed over and drew him into an embrace. "Good Lord, you had us all worried."

Elliot grabbed him by the shoulders. "Thankfully, I was oblivious to the event," he said with a smile.

Evelyn came over and threw her arms around him. She looked up into his eyes. "I am so pleased to see you." Her voice sounded croaky. The emotion of the last few days had been too much for all of them.

Elliot placed a brotherly hand to her cheek. "I hear we are to increase our numbers. Grace said we need two carriages to take our brood home."

Alexander's mouth curled up into an amused grin. "It seems I had no need to worry about spending my life alone."

Ivana touched him on the shoulder. "Come and meet the children."

She led him over to the bed, to the five pairs of wide eyes all staring at him with a look of wonder. Ivana introduced them, starting with the girls. Frederick and Edwin jumped down from the bed and offered the lord their most regal bow, just as she had taught them to do.

"Thank you, my lord," Frederick began, "for considering that we might come to England to live with Christoph. We do not want to be parted from our brother."

Ivana noted Elliot's gaze shift to the little boy on the bed, and he inhaled deeply before turning to the older boys. "I understand completely. You are both more than welcome to come and live with us if that is what you want."

"We do," Edwin said, blinking rapidly.

"Then I wish to welcome you both." Elliot opened his arms. Both boys hesitated, looked at each other and smiled before stepping forward to embrace him.

Ivana's throat hurt from suppressing a wealth of emotion. She moved to the bed and hauled Christoph up into her arms.

"Come, children," Evelyn said, "let us all go to my chamber and continue with our story."

There were cheers and chuckles and soon only Ivana, Elliot and Christoph were left in the room.

Elliot stared at the boy she held close. "I see a definite similarity in the eyes."

"And the hair, and the lips and ears by all accounts." She stroked Christoph's mop of ebony locks. "Do you wish to tell him the nature of your relationship or would you prefer to wait until the sun rises?"

He remained silent for a moment. "I shall explain the connection once we are home."

Ivana nodded. "Of course." She cuddled the boy, knowing it would be a long time before she got the chance to do so again. "You will be going to England, Christoph," she said as she kissed the child on the cheek. "You will live in a grand house with Lord and Lady Markham. Would you like that?"

Christoph's emerald eyes lit up, but he did not answer. Instead, he held his arms out to Elliot, who scooped the boy to his chest and held him there for the longest time. Guilt threatened to flare again, for the pain she had caused him, but she stamped it down knowing her intervention had served to lead him to his destined path.

"Would you like to come and live with me in England?" Elliot's voice sounded fractured, the pitch unusually high. When Christoph nodded, Elliot kissed him on his head, closed his eyes and breathed deeply.

Grace appeared at the door. "I hope I am not disturbing you."

Elliot shook his head. "Not at all. This moment would not be the same without you."

She rushed over to him, and he draped his arm around her shoulder.

"I shall leave you all in peace." Ivana inclined her head. She had achieved all she had set out to do for the children. The Bruhns were part of her family, and she would continue to give them her support. But now it was time to be selfish. "I shall go and find Leo. There is something important I must ask him."

Elliot stared at her, his gratitude reflected in his eyes. "Thank you," he said quietly, "for everything."

"Take care of my beautiful boys." She had confidence in their ability to provide a good and loving home. "Raise them to be honest men, to appreciate all that they have, to give to those who are not as fortunate."

Grace smiled. "We will continue the work you have begun. We promise you that."

Ivana knew if she spoke the tears would fall, and she had shed a lifetime's worth of tears in the space of a few days. Offering them a smile, she left the room and went in search of Leo.

She found him sitting against the wall on the floor in the crypt. His eyes were closed. Had he been human she would have assumed he was asleep.

"What are you doing down here?" she asked as she came to sit at his side. She put her head on his shoulder, threw her arm around his waist.

"It has been a wild few days," he said, rubbing her arm in soothing strokes. "I wanted to take a moment to gather my thoughts."

Ivana could feel the strange mixture of emotions swirling around in his chest. She looked up at him. "While you are happy that your brothers no longer suffer from the affliction, I sense that you do not want them to leave." She would not want him to stay with her out of obligation. "If you want to go home with them, you know I would understand." She would be devastated; the pain would be unbearable.

Leo jerked his head in surprise. His frantic gaze searched her face. "Do you want me to go?"

How could he even think such a thing?

"Leo, I am in love with you. I never want to be without you. But I want you to be happy, and I can see what your family mean to you."

He tugged her arm, pulled her to sit astride him. "Yes, I will miss them. But you are the most important person in my life." He placed his hands on her shoulders, gave a sinful smile as they drifted down to caress her breasts. "I love you and never want to be without you."

Unable to suppress the surge of desire, she rubbed against him. "Perhaps you should show me how much you want to stay. As creatures of the night, we will have to find something to occupy us during the day."

He raised a sinful brow as his hand skirted beneath the hem of her dress to massage her bare thigh. "Only during the day?"

She sucked in a breath as his fingers crept higher. "At night, we will behave like other humans. We will play cards in the tavern. I will watch you while you drink Herr Bruhn's ale. We will walk back through the forest. You can love me beneath the canopy of stars."

"And during the day, we will lock ourselves in a dark chamber, indulge our deepest desires."

"Yes," she breathed softly, as he stroked the place throbbing for his touch.

"But it is night now, Ivana. There are no stars in here and yet I so desperately want to be deep inside you." His nimble fingers mimicked the action he spoke of. "Does that mean we must wait until morning?"

Shamelessly, she pressed against his wicked hand. Her body ached for him. "No," she said, her mind becoming hazy, "but you must be quick before someone finds us."

She did not have to repeat the request. Within a few seconds, he'd unbuttoned his breeches and had anchored her to his hard body. With her palms placed flat on the wall behind his head, she rode him to completion.

"Now you're a widow, I suggest we marry," he said as his hands settled on her hips to hold her in place. He was still buried inside her, and she was reluctant to move.

"Are you suggesting it, or are you asking me?" She'd had every intention of broaching the subject, had even considered asking him. Besides, she was not a widow. According to Nikolai they had never married.

He held on to her while he raised his hips and pushed deeper inside. The sensation caused a ripple of desire. "Marry me, Ivana. Say you will be my wife."

She smiled, bent her head and kissed him. "I love you. I can barely breathe when I think of a life without you. Of course I'll marry you. It would be an honour to take your name, Leo."

"Perhaps we should mark the occasion with a toast." By the glint in his eye, she knew he had salacious thoughts. His gaze fell to her neck. "Perhaps you should lock the door as we wouldn't want anyone to witness the event."

The thought of drinking from him caused the muscles in her core to grip his growing manhood. "I would love to quench my thirst but may not stop at just a mouthful."

He raised an arrogant brow. "You won't hear me complain."

$\approx$

After a blissful, lust-fuelled hour spent in the crypt, Ivana and Leo joined the rest of the party in the Great Hall. Ivana was interested to hear the stories of how both brothers had met their wives. Understanding the nature of Grace's sister's plight explained why she had readily accepted Elliot's illegitimate son. Ivana did not tell them about the night Nikolai robbed her of her innocence. She had no desire to speak of him again. Instead, she listened to Leo tell of the night they had stood opposite each other in the rain, when he had threatened her with his mighty sword to avenge his friends.

As soon as the sun peeked up above the horizon, Elliot ventured outside. Based on the quantity of food he had eaten at dinner, Ivana had no doubt the cure had worked. Indeed, Julia informed her that the lord was lying sprawled out on the cobblestoned courtyard, staring up at the blue sky and wearing a grin that stretched from ear to ear.

While Elliot, Alexander, and their wives took the children to play outside, Ivana and Leo hid themselves away in their chamber and played a few games of their own that lasted until sunset.

For obvious reasons, the party chose to depart for England in the evening. Herr Bruhn came out to wave them off.

"I cannot feel sad tonight," he said to Ivana. "They all look so happy and will have the security of a loving family."

Ivana put her arm around his shoulder as she watched Leo hug his brothers. "It is all we ever wanted for them. I have spoken to Leo, and we would like you to think about coming to live in the castle." It meant she would have to compel them to forget certain things. Julia and Sylvester would care for the old couple during the day, and she could spend time with them in the evening.

"Well, I do not know what to say. Surely when you are married, you will not want to be lumbered with guests."

"You are like family, and you would have a wing of the castle to yourselves. Julia and Sylvester would relish the company. Oh, say you will consider it."

The old man nodded numerous times. "Of course, of course."

After they had all hugged each other too many times to count, Leo came to stand at Ivana's side. "Now, look after Chambers," Leo said to Alexander in reference to his coachman. "He is not used to taking instruction from a grumpy lord."

Alexander smirked. "Have no fear. I am far more content of late and not nearly as irritable." He inclined his head, but his cheerful countenance became more sorrowful. "We will find a way to be together soon. That is if I can stand to spend another three weeks confined to a carriage."

Ivana could feel Leo's pain as they watched the carriages rumble out of the village. She took his hand and held it tight.

Leo gave a heavy sigh. "We shall escort you home, Herr Bruhn."

Ivana glanced up as she felt the first drop of rain land on her skin. "Quick. You must get inside before you get wet and catch a chill."

Herr Bruhn's eyes widened. "But what of you? You cannot walk back to the castle in this terrible weather."

Leo glanced at her, a sinful smile playing at the corners of his mouth. "We enjoy walking out at night. Come. We will see you inside and then be on our way."

Herr Bruhn did not object. Perhaps he sensed their need to be alone. By the time they had reached the path leading up through the forest, their clothes were soaked through.

Leo held her hand tight. "Walking home like this, rouses similar feelings of a night spent together."

"Do you mean the night I lured a licentious rake from the tavern or the night you wanted to kill me?"

"Neither of those," he said thoughtfully. "I speak of another place, another lifetime. I feel as though I have travelled this path with you before. This is not the first time we have been hopelessly in love. I feel as though this was destined to be."

Ivana smiled. She, too, felt infinitely part of something much bigger than anything either of them could comprehend. "I have always felt that way. I have no doubt we would have found each other, eventually."

"Having witnessed how all our lives have changed in the last few months, I truly believe that now." He sighed. "I just wish my brothers did not live so far away."

Her heart ached for him. "I know. Despite the distance, we must hope that they will come and visit."

"I have been thinking that perhaps we could go to London. Not now, of course, but in the future. I know our affliction would make the journey difficult, but Elliot and Alexander managed it without incident."

Ivana did not want to disappoint him. "Perhaps, but we must accept that it might not be possible."

"No one knows what the future holds. You told me that." Leo stopped walking and turned to face her. He brought her hand to his lips and kissed it tenderly, his heated gaze locking with hers. "I am not a man who gives up easily."

His rich tone caused a tingle down the length of her spine. The rain trickled down their faces; their clothes clung to their skin, but she had not a single care in the world. Her heart was full, her soul sated. Her one true love stood with her, and she would do anything to make him happy.

"I don't doubt that when you set your mind to something you will not stop until you succeed," she said. "And you know I will support you in whatever you decide to do." She glanced up at the canopy of trees, at the thick black clouds peeking through gaps in the foliage and smiled. "But now it seems that the stars have chosen to shine brightly down upon us."

A sinful smile touched his lips, but he did not look to the heavens. "Standing beneath such a brilliant blanket can mean only one thing. We might not have played cards in the tavern or supped on Herr Bruhn's ale, but I think I can manage the other activity you suggested."

"You do not mind loving me in the rain?"

He glanced back over his shoulder at the sturdy tree trunk. "I'm surprised you even need to ask."

EPILOGUE

LONDON, 1822

"Good Lord. How much longer must we stay here?" Alexander complained, exhaling loudly.

Elliot chuckled as he scanned the crowded ballroom. "Have you forgotten that this is your house? As you're the host and are supposed to be celebrating Aunt Beatrice's return from India, I estimate all night."

"Bloody hell," Alexander muttered. "Remind me to be a little firmer with Evelyn in future."

Elliot shrugged. "Well, there is one consolation."

"What is it? I cannot think of any reward great enough to compensate for an evening spent having meaningless conversations with dim-wits."

"Is not Evelyn's gratitude reward in itself? I would wager you're not half as annoyed as you make yourself out to be."

The corners of Alexander's mouth twitched in amusement. "Evelyn finds it immensely satisfying to know she has the power to soothe my tortured soul."

Elliot scanned the sea of heads gracing the dance floor. "I would have a care. That is the second dance she has shared with Mr. Hartwood's nephew." Elliot enjoyed teasing his friend. "Perhaps the gentleman is as besotted as you are."

Alexander's expression darkened. "It will be the last dance he shares with anyone if he so much as looks at her inappropriately."

Elliot spotted Grace waltzing with Lord Walton. A dazzling smile illuminated her face; a few fiery red curls brushed against the smooth column of her neck. Damn. Would there ever be a day when he would not be consumed with thoughts of bedding his own wife?

"I'm afraid we've no option but to dance with our wives," Elliot said, feeling a desperate need to hold Grace in his arms. "I once overheard a gentleman telling his partner that dancing is a prelude to seduction. I suggest you use the opportunity to brush up your skills."

Alexander raised an arrogant brow. "There is nothing wrong with—"

A commotion at the far end of the room captured their attention, the excited chatter audible above the music filling the air.

Elliot tutted. "There is always someone who deliberately arrives late in a bid to command attention." He patted Alexander on the upper arm. "As the host, you should go and greet them."

"Shush," Alexander said with an irate glare. "I've no desire to spend another moment feigning interest in feathers and fripperies."

Elliot craned his neck, hoping to direct the new arrivals his way. Well, he had to find some way to amuse himself. Watching Alexander squirm always proved entertaining.

As he watched an array of heads part to make a pathway through the throng, a strange feeling of familiarity flooded his chest. As soon as he glimpsed the lady's golden locks and the gentleman's brown hair, his heart skipped a beat.

Elliot narrowed his gaze.

Leo?

His friend's face filled his field of vision. Elliot's mind told him it was impossible, that his eyes were seeing a glittering mirage concocted by his wild imagination.

"Good Lord," he gasped, blinking rapidly out of fear he had made a mistake. "Leo is here."

"Don't be absurd," Alexander said, turning to scan the room. "They'd not travel all the way—"

As the couple broke through the crowd, Leo and Ivana were suddenly standing before them. Elliot's heart almost leapt through his mouth. Without another word he raced over, embraced his brother, brought his sister's hand to his lips and kissed it. Alexander came to join them, his cries of joy attracting attention.

"What the hell are you doing here?" Elliot struggled to contain his excitement. The blood rushed through his body so quickly he could hear it vibrating in his ears.

Leo grinned. "We've come to rescue you from the evil clutches of a room full of bores."

Ivana tapped Leo playfully on the arm. "We have come to stay for a while."

Alexander cleared his throat. "Having braved the three-week journey, you'll need to stay for a month to recuperate."

Ivana glanced at Leo and smiled. "I think we plan to stay a little longer than that."

Ignoring the gapes and stares, they bombarded the new arrivals with questions. As soon as the dance ended, Evelyn and Grace hurried over, and they spent another few minutes embracing.

"And so now you are a marchioness," Evelyn said affectionately.

"As I have just been reminded by those who stopped to greet us," Ivana replied. "You know what it is like at the castle. No one pays any notice to such things."

Leo raised a brow. "From your most recent letter, I understand we have two new nephews."

All four of them tried to answer at once, but then stopped, laughed and gestured for Elliot to continue. "Our sons are both six months old."

"Louis is our son." Grace beamed with pride.

"And Theo is ours," Evelyn added.

"And what of the other children," Ivana asked eagerly. "Are they well? Are they thriving?"

Elliot nodded. "They are all doing remarkably well. Come to Portman Square tomorrow evening." He had almost invited them for dinner but thankfully remembered that they still suffered from the affliction. "We will all gather there and wait until you're able to venture out."

Ivana smiled. "That would be wonderful. I cannot wait to see their smiling faces."

"How … how are the Bruhns?" Evelyn asked hesitantly.

"They are living up at the castle," Leo informed. "Herr Bruhn carves wooden figures. He has made one for each of the children."

"Come," Alexander said. "Let us go and find somewhere quiet to talk, where there are not twenty pairs of ears all listening out for a juicy piece of gossip."

As they made their way through the ballroom in a bid to reach Alexander's study before being pounced upon by another nosey guest, Elliot gave a contented sigh. It felt good to be together again. In his wildest dreams, he would never have thought the golden-haired devil would become like a sister to him. Life had a way of delivering the unexpected. Even in the darkest times, he now knew one must always have faith.

～

The next morning, Leo woke with a start as he struggled to recognise his surroundings. It took him a moment to realise he was in London and not snuggled up in their huge bed in the castle.

The warm body curled next to him shuffled closer. "What time is it?" Ivana asked dreamily.

Leo glanced around the room. "I haven't the faintest idea. Sometime before noon, I would hazard a guess."

Ivana stretched her arms above her head, the soft curve of her breasts rising up to meet his greedy gaze. "I don't know about you, but I hardly slept a wink. My mind kept replaying various scenarios. Will the children look the same? Will they remember me?"

"Of course they will remember you." He caressed her cheek, gave a mischievous grin when his hand drifted lower. "Perhaps you need to find a way to occupy your mind, an activity to make you forget your fears."

From her sinful smile, he knew she was just as eager as he to partake in a little vigorous exercise. "Is there ever a morning when you are not in an amorous mood?"

Leo thought for a moment. "No. Not since meeting you."

"As your wife, I believe it is my duty to oblige."

"Good Lord, you know how to dampen a man's ardour." He felt soft fingers circle his throbbing cock. "Then again, I find I quite like your approach."

Two hours later, while the sun shone brightly in the sky,

Leo and Ivana stood in the hall of their townhouse in Cavendish Square.

"I still get nervous at the thought of stepping outside," she said as she tied the ribbons on her bonnet.

Leo nodded. "After years of hiding in the shadows, I think we will never feel completely at ease in the sun."

"What do you think they will say when they see us?" Ivana clapped her hands, her excitement evident on her face.

"I have no idea," he chuckled. "Perhaps swoon in shock."

Leo opened the front door. They hovered on the threshold, let the rays of light infuse their being.

"Well, I cannot hear sizzling. That is always a good sign." Leo offered his arm, and Ivana hugged it tight. "Shall we go and surprise our friends?"

"Yes, my love." Ivana nodded confidently. "Let us go and share our good fortune."

They walked the half mile to Portman Square. After years of living in the dark, they took every opportunity to feel the sun warm their skin. Once there, they discovered that Elliot, Grace, and the children had joined Alexander, Evelyn and their children in the park for a picnic.

After a twenty-minute stroll around the park, they noticed their friends sitting on the grass, nibbling on food laid out on a blanket. The children were running around, laughing and giggling and Leo knew the sight would bring a tear to Ivana's eye.

"They all look so happy, Leo," she said, her voice sounding a little shaky. "I feel as though my heart is about to burst from my chest."

Indeed, he felt the same way too. To see the sun beating down upon his brothers' smiling faces was perhaps one of the most splendid things he had ever witnessed.

As they crept closer, Frederick glanced in their direction. He stopped and stared before his eyes grew wide and round.

"Frau Lockwood. Frau Lockwood," he cried as he charged towards them.

Ivana picked up the hem of her skirt and rushed towards the boy, scooping him up in her arms and hugging him tight.

Elliot and Alexander jumped up from the grass. They stared at Leo for the longest time and then they, too, ran towards him, picking him up and cheering loudly.

Despite numerous frowns and complaints from passersby, no one cared. In their excitement, they all ended up in a heap on the grass.

"Please tell me I am not dreaming," Elliot said, gasping for breath.

"No. You're not dreaming." Leo could feel his smile stretching from ear to ear. "It only took me two blasted years to replicate Talliano's elixir. I doubt there is a rat alive in all of Bavaria." He turned to Alexander. "You'll be pleased to know I am now an expert in deciphering illegible Latin."

"You should have known he would not give up so easily," Ivana added before being swamped by the children's eagerness to embrace her.

Elliot's gaze drifted over him. "Did you suffer as we did?"

Leo shivered as the memory surfaced. "Once my most recent batch had proved successful, Ivana took it first. I managed to compel her to sleep."

"I begged him to take it before me, but he would not listen," Ivana said.

"It was horrendous," Leo groaned. "With no one to compel me to sleep, I writhed on the floor in agony for hours, but the end result was more than worth the pain."

Elliot sighed. "Well, you are here to tell the tale."

Leo winced as he recalled their recent adventure in Scotland. Damn it. They had almost been bitten again.

Ivana turned to Christoph, who was sitting next to Grace. "Do you remember me, Christoph? Do you remember your time in Bavaria?"

The child shook his head. Leo knew Ivana had spent many days and nights worrying about the boy.

"Do you not remember when we were at the castle?" Grace said softly. "We rode in a carriage all the way home and Edwin had a stomach ache for days."

Christoph's eyes widened. "Yes, mama, I think I do."

Ivana gasped and put her hand to her heart. She opened her mouth a few times but struggled to speak.

"So I assume your three-week journey was not as treacherous as I suspected," Alexander said.

"We did not come here directly," Leo informed. "We spent time in Scotland before venturing south."

"Scotland?" Elliot repeated. "What on earth were you doing there?"

"It's a long story, but I shall tell you about it this evening. For now, let us relish the time we have together. I never thought I would ever see the day when we would all be sitting together like this."

A few people stopped and stared as they all lay on the grass smiling up at the cloudless sky. For no reason at all, Elliot chuckled loudly, the contagious sound leaving them all in fits of laughter. They held hands, the physical bond a sign of the love they shared. They were a family. Nothing would ever break the bond of the brotherhood.

The End

Made in the USA
Middletown, DE
14 July 2019